## ABOUT THE AUTHOR

Dominic Lyne has suffered from psychosis since the age of four, and has been diagnosed with Schizotypal Disorder, Dissociative Disorder, and Borderline Personality Disorder. All of these mental health issues bleed into his work through his creation of claustrophobic landscapes and offer the reader an insight into his world, the world he has created and mutated in his physical reality.

www.dom-lyne.co.uk

# The Heart of Darkness

# The Heart of Darkness

## Dominic Lyne

ARTEMIS PUBLISHERS

© Copyright 2014 Dominic Lyne

The right of Dominic Lyne to be identified as author of
This work has been asserted by him in accordance with the
Copyright, Designs and Patents Act 1988

**All Rights Reserved** No part of this publication may be reproduced,
stored or transmitted in any form without written permission of the
publisher. Any person who does any unauthorised act in relation to
This publication may be liable to criminal prosecution and civil
claims for damage.

All characters and places are fictitious and any similarity
is purely unintentional.

ISBN-978-1-907785-17 7

**First Published in 2014**

ARTEMIS PUBLISHERS LTD.

Hamilton House
Mabledon Place
Bloomsbury
London
WC1H 9BB

**www.artemispublishers.com**

Printed & Bound in Great Britain

# DEDICATION

*For Tree, you'll always be the light in my darkness.*

# CONVERSATION I

# ONE

The body was cold before it even hit the ground. Its corpse lays there empty of all that had once filled it, made it what it was. The blood mixes with the tears of the gutter and pools a dirty crimson.

He looks at it in silence. Words had murdered it; actions had been the aftermath. Words. The mouth had opened without thought; without care he had spat out the venom of anger and they burnt their acid holes into the veil of reality. The scene changed its tone. Everything ended.

Love had died.

'I'm sorry,' he says.

Silence.

'I'm so fucking sorry.'

Silence.

'We have already been over this part, Daniel,' she says gently, pulling her glasses off her face and holding them by one leg. 'This is how we always start. We need to move on from here.'

'You don't understand. How could you?' Daniel rocks gently in his seat, hunched up, his knees against his chin, mouth chewing at his nails. He makes eye contact. 'How the *fuck* could you?'

'Help me to understand. That is why I am here.' With a sigh she pushes her glasses back onto her face, repositions herself and makes notes on the pad that had been resting on her knee. Her nails are painted red.

'Why do you need to understand?'

'I don't, but you do. We need to find the root of all this. Then you can move on. Some things are best not holding on to.'

He rocks faster.

'Calm down, Daniel.'

'I'm sorry,' he whispers.

She says nothing.

'I'm so sorry.'

Nothing.

The rocking stops. He looks her in the eye and curls his lip. 'Why don't you fucking say something? Why does no one ever say anything at that point?'

'It is not for me to forgive you.'

'I don't want your forgiveness.'

'No, you need your own.'

'Bitch.'

'Daniel, I am not here to hurt you, nor damage your memories. We need a common ground.'

'Why? So you can fuck with my head? Change me?' He snorts a laugh. 'Save me?'

'Do you need saving?'

'You tell me.'

Her pen scratches against paper. 'So, tell me about the start.'

'Start of what?'

'The beginning, your earliest memory where you can now pinpoint your condition.'

'Condition? You make me sound like a machine.'

'I am sorry, I will rephrase. Tell me your earliest memory where you felt that you were different from your contemporaries.'

'I've always felt different.'

'Okay, then pick a memory. The earliest one.'

'An angry one?'

'Only if you think it is relevant.'

He sits in silence for a minute. Searching through the battlefield of his mind. Searching through his past as a computer searches for file names. One is selected. He pushes the video into the machine and presses play.

The butterfly flaps around gracefully. Its wings the purest white. He follows it, chasing its erratic path, laughing to himself as he does so. It rests on a bright red flower and closes its wings together, unaware of his approach. He jumps and cups his hands around it. It tickles his palms as it tries to escape its prison. He laughs, flattens his palms together and tightens their vice like grip. He hears a crunch; he feels nothing.

The butterfly's crushed body is left to rot in the long grass as he bounds off after another one. Forgotten, dead. A memory that has already been lost. His mind elsewhere, he jumps, becomes careless and all the others escape into the blue sky, rising like snowflakes in reverse.

Then the rain came. The storm clouds had flooded in so quietly and unnoticed that the torrential outpouring they vomited down upon the earth caught him by surprise. The sky had darkened, lightning had forked and the thunder trembled through him. His eyes cast to the heavens, he sees. The figure in the clouds, the shadow staring down upon him, opening its heart, spewing forth tendrils of darkness that reach down to caress him with their icy touch. His mother's cries for him to return to the car just whispers on the edge of his consciousness. Insignificant to the splendour his eyes witness. Another roll of thunder, deeper, bringing with it the music of the shadows; the low hum, ebbing and flowing around him, pushing its way into his soul.

Arms wrap around him. A scolding voice in his ears as he is lifted from his feet and hurried away. Over the shoulder of his mother, he continues to stare into the shadow. He stares into the heart of darkness. He stares into oblivion, and it stares back at him.

'So how old were you when you saw that?' she asks clinically.

'Probably around three years old.'

'And you remember it so clearly?'

'It gets replayed a lot.'

'Replayed?'

'So vividly that it's like I'm reliving it.'

'Watching yourself?'

'No, seeing through my own eyes. Smelling the static air with my own nose. It's like there's a rip in reality and I slip through it and am transported back to that moment, it's more than just a memory.'

'What do you think you saw in those clouds?'

'It tried to show me my soul.'

She scribbles on her pad. 'Your soul? Explain that to me.'

'It feels like I'm looking...'

'Was.'

'Pardon?'

'It felt like you were…'

'No, *is*. Every time I see it, it feels real. *Is* real. When I stand there looking up I see the shadow showing me my soul. My being stripped of all its decaying flesh and bone. What I am. Who I am. My soul.'

'So you believe it shows you that you have a "heart of darkness"?'

'Don't we all? Don't we all have a dark side, a selfish side? A side that wants to punch, kill, destroy. A side that will watch all of those and do nothing to prevent it, gains pleasure from it.'

'You believe that?'

'Don't you?'

'To some extent. It is human nature, but most of us don't embrace it, we hate ourselves for it.'

'Why hate your nature?'

'Do you not dislike it?'

He doesn't answer.

'Daniel?'

'It's part of who I am. I can't control it. In that moment I looked into oblivion, I felt its touch empty me, then I saw my soul. I'm empty. Always fucking empty.' His voice breaks and he cries. 'Please help me,' he pleads between sobs. 'Help me. Please.'

She pushes the box of tissues on the table towards him. She knows they won't help. They never do. It's just an act of professional habit. 'If you want, we can take a break. Let you compose yourself. Go for a cigarette. Would you like that?'

He nods.

'Okay, let's take ten minutes.'

He leaves the room without saying another word, wiping his eyes on his sleeve. The door closes behind him. She writes on her pad.

# TWO

'How are you feeling?' she asks upon his return, noting the stale aroma of cigarette smoke. 'Are you ready to continue?'

He nods.

'Okay. You said you feel empty. How do you mean empty?'

'I guess you'd say it's like I'm a ghost; I don't exist. Well, I do exist, but only by myself, incomplete and ignored.'

'Incomplete?'

'Like there's something missing, something just isn't there at my core and in its place is this hollow empty hole that sucks everything else into it. Draining me until I'm like a fragile crystal glass. Then I just wait for that final knock, the tipping and shattering into thousands of pieces.'

'Has that happened?'

'Always.'

'What do you do then?'

'Put myself back together again as best I can. What else can you do? Each time one piece is lost but you just carry on.'

'So each time you become more fragile and incomplete?'

'Yes.'

'What sits at the heart of this emptiness?'

'The darkness.'

'The darkness?'

'The darkness, oblivion. The despair of eternity. The endless suffering without redemption.'

'Redemption? Do you feel that that is necessary?'

'It's a form of hope, a way to prove all the suffering has meant something.'

'You need to be saved?'

'You tell me.' He looks down at the floor.

'You said you needed help.'

'Are "help" and "saved" the same things?'

'Not always.'

'So are their needs independent of each other?'

'You mentioned redemption.'

'No I said "without redemption." No hope.'

'Okay, I think I understand.' Her pen scratches on paper. Slowly she sits back in her chair, watching him, mentally surveying his movements. 'So what happened after your mother got you safely back to the car? Did she ever mention it?'

'It was never mentioned again.'

'Do you think she saw it?'

'If she did she never said.'

'Did you, or have you asked her about it?'

'I just said it was never mentioned again.'

'So you never spoke about it?'

He gets visibly agitated. 'I just told you didn't I? It was my moment, whether she saw it or not is irrelevant. I saw it, that's all that matters.'

'You were three; could it not have been part of your imagination? You wanted it to be true.'

'I *was* true and it *did* happen.'

'Daniel, part of your disorder allows for this. Somewhere you have learnt to create images, people who embody the fractured parts of your emotions. You create physical representations of them.'

'I did not create it.'

'They may seem real to you,' she continues without acknowledging his words. 'But they have no real basis.'

'It was not a hallucination.'

'How can you be sure?'

'It was real. In my world it was real. It existed. It happened. Who the hell are you to say otherwise?'

'Daniel, you are sick and we need to ascertain when this disorder first presented itself.'

'You tell me it's a fucking disorder, but this is my life. This is how it has always been. Who are you to come in and tell me it's not real? Who the fuck are you to judge based solely on what *you've* experienced or not?'

'I am the help you have been seeking all your life.'

'I have never searched for help. No one can help me.'

'That is true. Only you can help yourself, but I can help you do that.'

'I'm damaged. I'm broken. What good am I?'

'You are a beautiful person and the only one who cannot see that is you.'

He snorts a laugh. 'What the fuck do you know?'

'Daniel...' She sighs and lets the sentence hang incomplete in the air, weighing it down like lead. Her mind seeking the next logical direction in which to take the session. He may be a person, but he is also a patient, a statistic. A problem that needs to be solved.

'The field was pretty,' Daniel starts without prompting. 'When the butterflies flew into the air it was as though everything was in reverse. Time breaking its natural laws and making a glorious middle finger at all those who believed the set in stone laws we are all expected to abide by. It felt as though that one small life I had crushed was given another chance to breathe again, that behind me it rose again and joined its brothers and vanished into the heavens, carefree and unaware. Time bent and it got a second chance.'

'Did it deserve it?'

'Deserve what?'

'A second chance.'

'Doesn't everything? Doesn't everyone?'

'I am sure some will disagree with you.'

'Why? Who has the right to say who is worthy enough for a second chance?'

'Who has the right to decide who lives and dies?'

Silence. His eyes say it all.

'Why did you kill it?'

'Because I could.'

'How did it make you feel?'

'Nothing.'

Her pen scribbles on the pad.

'Giving you the answers you need?' he asks.

'There are no set answers, you know this. All I ask is that you are truthful.'

'Truth is all I can say.'

'Then truth is all I can write.'

'Truth with opinion.'

'Everyone will always have an opinion.'

'True.' He bites his fingernail. 'Then truth can be questioned.'

'Sometimes. You are diverting away from where we are meant to be going. Tell me, after seeing it in the sky, when was the next time you saw the shadow?'

'He was with me from that day on.'

'So tell me your next memory.'

The room is dark. Darker than usual. He is curled up in bed, the covers pulled tightly around him. His eyes stare out of the window, trying to catch a glimpse of the stars but God had tuned out the lights and all he can see is the inky black of infinity.

'Daniel.' The voice is a whisper. He jumps at its sound, pulls the blanket tighter around him. He tries to pinpoint its source. He can't so he waits for a repeat. It comes and it sounds familiar. He hears it in his head, disembodied from his usual thought processes. If his 'self' is in a room controlling his form, then this voice comes from behind him. A cold shiver. Behind him means the wall.

He flips round and stares at the blank white. Nothing there. He rolls onto his back, breathing deeply.

'Daniel.' Behind him. That means below him.

He wants to cry. Cry like the child he is, but he doesn't. His name is said again and he looks to his left at his wardrobe. Its door is open a crack, it causes him to swallow. It's escaped. That means…

The room grows darker. The shadows creeping in upon the natural shadows that already existed. Something moves below him. A scratching against the frame of the bed. He pulls the blankets off slowly and leans over the side and looks beneath. He makes eye contact and he knows. The shadow stares back at him; even on its side he knows it's tall, gaunt. They look at each other in silence for what seems like an eternity but what in reality is a split second before the scared boy hides himself under his covers.

Minutes pass and he braves another look. Under the bed is just the usual mess of his discarded toys. He sighs in relief and looks back out at the starless night. On their journey back to the window, his eyes notice the wardrobe door is closed. He chooses not to react.

'So, the shadow "lived" in the wardrobe?' she asks.

'That was usually where I'd see it.'

'Was it caged?'

'No, the wardrobe was in a corner. It likes corners. The wardrobe was always in shadow, it was always dark.'

'So it likes the dark?'

'Of course it does.' He looks at her as though she is thick. 'It's a shadow, it's hardly gonna stand around in the sun is it?'

'The sun creates shadows.'

'Shadows of objects. It is the object; it creates the darkness. It is its own shadow.'

'Do you think you have lived in the shadows?'

'All outsiders live in the shadows of society. We all group together in the places nobody looks.'

'So you hide?'

'We don't hide from you, you stay in the light away from us. You don't understand us so you shun us.'

'Like you shun society?'

'Society isolated us first so why are we expected to take the blame? You forced us into the shadows because you couldn't deal with us. How is that our fault?'

'We try to understand you.'

'You try to change us. Mutate us to your will.'

'Help you.'

'Help us to be a part of *your* world. You dismiss ours as fake.'

'You need to see reality. That is all we try to do.'

'*Your* reality. Why is ours so alien to you? Why do you fear it? Why is it considered unacceptable just because it goes against yours? What makes yours so right?'

'There are certain ways that make the brain function correctly.'

'By your standards. I think it's because our world challenges yours, challenges all the safety nets you've put up as protection from the unknown. We see what you fear and as a result we must be altered. What if I'm right?'

'In your mind you might be.'

'No, what if I'm right and you are all wrong? You never think that do you? By your standards Jesus would have a disorder but look at the effect he had on the world.'

'Are you comparing yourself to Jesus?'

'No, I'm just saying one man can change a lot.'

'Science has countered religion.'

'No, science has overthrown God and placed its logic as the divine deity. It is still just a questionable belief. It only justifies what is known. It has no control over the unknown and that is why it dismisses it.'

She moves uncomfortably in her chair. 'We are not here to discuss the ethics and reasons of science, Daniel.'

'Does it make you uncomfortable?'

'It is not why you are here.'

He doesn't say anything, just stares off into space. His mind stumped by the abrupt halt of its direction.

'Stay with it, Daniel.' She leans forward. 'We need to make progress.'

He nods slowly.

'Okay. Do you think the presence of the shadow changed who you were?'

'I was three. I can only remember how I was past that, but to answer your question, no, no I don't think it did. I just carried on how I always did, there was no dramatic *Exorcist* style mutation of my character.'

'That you remember.'

'Are you going to question everything I say? Dismiss it as if you know better? You want me to tell the truth, I do, but then you twist it into a lie. You make out that I'm not in control of my own opinions.'

'But...'

'Don't even go there, even if they are based on a "disorder", they are no less true in both my world and yours. If you're going to make me feel like a liar, or a retard who has no control, then this is over. If you want lies, I can give you them if it makes your job easier.'

'I'm trying to get a picture of who you are.'

'No, you're mutating it into the picture of what you want me to be. So to repeat the answer to your question: No, I don't think it did.'

'Okay.' She scribbles away on her pad furiously. 'So where do *you* what to take this? What do you feel is important about that memory or any other you've mentioned?'

'Their beauty. Each one has a beauty about it. The butterflies, the starless sky. The depth of infinity and the unknown. You can get lost in them.'

'Is that why they are so comforting to return to?'

'I guess so. In each, no matter what my initial emotion is, I know it won't harm me.'

'Daniel, can we for the sake of record refer to these memories in the past tense, not how you relive them? I want to know what you first thought not re-evaluated.'

'Okay. I knew it was part of me somehow.' He pauses, and rolls words through his mind. 'I thought we were opposites; that it was the dark to my innocence, connected but at that point untouched.'

'And now?'

'Now it watches over me. Guides, directs. It oversaw my loss of innocence. It is to be feared.'

'I think it is the personification of something you do not want to contain, so you externalise it.'

'How so?'

'It is like your anger or rage; that is why you say it must be feared. You do not want to feel its presence in you.'

'Don't or can't?'

'Both in equal measure. If you could it would destroy you, so you don't.'

'Interesting point,' he says.

'Professional observation.'

'Either way, there's an innocence in those memories. I was innocent to a point. Yes, I might have killed insects but I didn't know about the powers of life and death, or right and wrong. I just existed and did as I pleased.'

She says nothing, just writes.

'That's how I've always been. I do as I please.'

'Were there any consequences?'

'If there was I just shifted them so they passed me by unharmed. I've always been able to get myself out of trouble.'

'By manipulation?'

'If you want to label it as such. When I was younger I used to think it was by magic, but as I grew older I realised that that's all that magic is. True magic is manipulation.'

'Would you say you that you are good at it?'

'You tell me.'

'I think you are probably a master at it, and have been since an early age.'

'I don't know if that's a compliment.'

'I do not think it is in your case.'

'Oh.' *Bitch*, he thinks.

'When do you think the shadow corrupted you? No, let me rephrase that. When do you think the shadow begun to interfere with your experience?'

'Probably from that moment it first showed itself in the sky.'

'But you said it did not change you.'

'It didn't, it just began to make its presence known, and once it did I began to think about control. Not allowing myself to be pushed around, not being afraid of hurting people.'

'Does control result in hurt?'

'Of course it does. That is what control is. It doesn't have to be blatant, but someone has to lose something to the other's gain. I belong to no one but others do belong to me.'

'Are you in control now?'

'No, that's why I'm here.'

'Do you dislike not being in control?'

'I fucking hate it.'

'If the shadow "guides" you, does that not mean it has some control over you?'

'As I said, that is why I am here.'

'Okay, I am beginning to understand you better. Well, a bit of your nature.'

'Whatever.'

'I want to go back to that night you said the shadow was under your bed.' She sits back and gets comfortable.

'Okay.'

'Continue.'

'What?'

'Continue the memory from where you left off.'

'Oh, right...'


He stares into the black oblivion of the night sky; even the moon dares not provide any illumination. The clouds non-existent. He knows he's looking into the depths of the eternal silence that surrounds his world.

He hears someone stir in the room next to him. He closes his eyes as his mother gets out of bed and moves through her room to the door. He hears her enter his room. She pauses on the threshold; he knows she's searching for something. She leaves and he hears her open all the doors as she travels through the house. She reaches the final room and opens the door. His brother is disturbed from his sleep and he listens to the whispered conversation.

'Go back to sleep,' Mother's voice says gently.
'What's wrong?'
'I saw something, it woke me up.'
'What did?'
'It doesn't matter.'
'Must of if you're walking around.'
'I saw someone's shadow leave my room. I saw it go into Daniel's room but there's nothing there.'
'Maybe it was him wandering about.'
'He's asleep, and it was too tall to be him. Must have been my imagination. Don't worry about it. Go to sleep.'

She closes his door and returns to her room. The house falls silent again. He falls asleep.

'There was someone under my bed last night,' Daniel whispers to his brother as they sit at the table for breakfast.
'Don't be silly.'
'There was. I'm telling you.'
'Who was it then?'
'I don't know. The wardrobe was open.'
'What did it look like?'
'Just all black, like a shadow. It was the size of my bed. It was looking at me.'
'Did you see its eyes?'
'No.'
'How do you know it was looking at you then?'
Daniel shrugs his shoulders. 'It was.'

'What did it do?'

'Just lay there. Then it was gone when I looked again.'

'And the wardrobe?'

'Shut.'

'Maybe it's the ghost.'

Daniel says nothing.

'Don't worry; I've heard you talking to something in the wardrobe. I've seen you do it.'

'No you haven't.'

'Have so. You sit there with the doors open talking to it.'

'Do not.' Daniel's voice rises in volume.

'You do! I've seen it.'

'Liar!'

'What?'

'You're a big fibber. I don't talk to anyone.'

Their mother enters the kitchen. 'What's going on?'

'He says I talk to myself,' Daniel says.

'I didn't.'

'Liar!' A shout.

'Daniel!' Mother. She looks at his brother. 'Leave him alone.'

'But I've seen him do it.'

'Enough! Just leave it and get on with your breakfast.' She leaves.

The two brothers glare at each other.

'Was he telling the truth?' she asks.

'I dunno. I don't remember talking to either myself or the shadow in the wardrobe.'

'So he could have been telling the truth?'
'Maybe. Who knows?'
'Do you think now that it was a possibility?'
Daniel shrugs. 'I haven't given it much thought.'
'Okay.' Notes are made.
'I always remember being aware it was there. Just never communicating with it. Not at that point anyway.'
'So you did?'
'Eventually.'
'Interesting.'
'Not really. "Inevitable" would be the word I'd use.'
'Inevitable?'
'Yeah, like when you see someone you like. It's inevitable you'll at least talk to them once at some point.' He pauses. 'Soon after that though was when I started drawing them.'
'After what?'
'That conversation.'
'Okay, and what did you start drawing exactly?'
'The monsters. The creatures. They just appeared in my head and I transferred their images into the real world.'
'What monsters?'
'The things I drew.'
'Where did you draw them?'
'On my wall. Only at night though, when everyone was asleep. They used to animate after I'd finished.'
'Did they interact with you?'
'Never. Only with themselves.'

# THREE

'There was quite a few of them,' he says. 'But they all fell under the authority of one.'

'Did it have a name?'

He smiles to himself and snorts a laugh. 'Yeah, a stupid childhood title.'

'Which was?'

'The Blib Blob.'

'The Blib Blob?' she repeats with clinical precision.

'Yeah, it was exactly that. A giant purple blob.'

'What did it do to the others?'

'Consumed them.'

'As in ate them?'

'No, it consumed them. It consumed everything that made them them. It grew after each one; absorbing everything.'

'What did it gain by doing so?'

'How would I know? I just witnessed the events. It played out like a film before my eyes. It would just attack, consume, then return to its lair.'

'You saw it?'

'Yes.'

'That is what you meant when you said it "animated"?'

'Yup. It would move of its own accord in 2D. Like watching a cartoon.'

'And it never communicated with you on any level?'

'I wasn't part of its world.'

'You where its creator.'

'I'm not God.'

'But you did create it by drawing it.'

'Its image appeared without thought. It just appeared in my head fully formed as if created by someone else.'

'Was it always drawn the same?'

'Always.'

'And what of the other monsters?' She leans forward intrigued. 'How did they appear in the morning?'

'They would be smears. Just smudges of what they used to be. Only the Blib Blob would remain as drawn.'

'Did you smear the others?'

'No. I would always be laid down watching. I never touched the wall after I'd drawn them.'

'Interesting.' The pen moves across paper. 'Why did you start drawing on the walls? Had you done it previously?'

'Dunno, and no. It all started with the Blib Blob.'

'Okay. Do you think there was any significance to the images?'

'If there was I've forgotten it. There might have been at the time.'

'Do you think it was triggered by the shadow?'

'It started soon after I'd seen it under the bed, but again I can't remember. It's now just fact, something that happened, all reasons have been lost to the memories of eternity.'

'So, if you can't remember the reasons for them, why did you mention it?'

'Because of how it ended.'

'Ended?'

'Yeah, it ended as instantly as it had begun. One final drawing, given it was massive, but after that night I never drew the Blib Blob again.'

'Never?'

'Never, I couldn't even remember how to or what it looked like. Its image vanished as quickly as it appeared. It appeared from nothing and disappeared into nothing.'

He doesn't know what has come over him. He draws as though he is in a trance. The crayons move and his mind is blank. Autopilot; controlled from afar by alien hands. He moves quietly in the darkness, pausing at every creak the house makes as it sleeps. If he gets caught he's in big trouble. No one disturbs him; no one interrupts or prevents its completion.

He steps back and looks at it for the first time. A map, a giant map scrawled on the entire length of the wall and as tall as he can reach. At the heart of it sits the Blib Blob. Tall and commanding it stares out at him, whilst all around it the other monsters fidget nervously or try to hide in their caves.

He sits down on the floor. His back against one door of the wardrobe; the other open next to him. He can feel the coldness from within it. Sees the shadow standing inside out of the corner of his eye, but his attention is on his creation. The world of monsters. He smiles. He gets comfortable. The Blib Blob begins to move.

Its form spreads like crude oil, spewing forth and engulfing everything. A volcano claiming land with its molten death. The land turns black under its growth. Trees burn, lakes evaporate. The land turns sterile in its wake.

The shadow of the monster's progress covering the land in darkness. Feeding off everything in its path, consuming, absorbing. Raping the world that gave it life and set it up at the top of its hierarchy. Head of the food chain. Devour. Devour. Everything is devoured. The land mass just a black ink spot on the wall. One giant being covering the entire surface. It stands triumphant. Looking at its empire of nothing in gluttonous silence.

Then it happens. With nothing left to consume it begins to consume itself. Starting at its edges, its insatiable hunger eats inwards. Devouring until there is nothing left. The mouth eats itself last without so much as a sound. How could it have made one? It had already eaten its vocal cords.

He stares at the blank wall. He stares at death.

'So the monster devoured itself?'

'It grew too big. Destroyed everything else. Once you've consumed everything, the only thing left to consume is yourself.'

'So it just vanished?'

'It ceased to exist. It became a memory.'

'And you could never draw it again after that?'

'Never. The best way to destroy a cancer is to remove any trace of its existence, even from your own mind. I imagine that's what God feels like when he creates and eliminates.'

'But you remember it.'

'Everything leaves a scar. It becomes a word with no images. A point of time that can't be erased or imagined. It just is. It just exists in its own nonexistence.'

'Did you ever wonder why you stopped?'

'It was a logical conclusion. I never felt the need to, the impulse to do so had gone.'

'Was it a phase?'

'You could describe it as that.'

'How would you describe it?'

'A period. A growth.' He rubs his arms. 'As to its relevance to what you want to know, then I don't know.'

'I actually think it is very relevant. It seems to have been the first visual insight into your view of the world.'

'How so?'

'The over consumption of humanity; the absorption of the weak. Control. Dominance. The dangers of both.'

'I was four when I drew that last picture. I doubt I was that aware.'

'I think you were, are, a highly intelligent person. You picked up at a very early age how to avoid and extend the boundaries to your world. I think you picked up a lot subconsciously and it grew as you became more aware of the real world you lived in.'

'If you say so.'

'An intelligent child with no boundaries is a very dangerous combination. You see, Daniel, these were not just images. You created a "living" existence in your head. You knew drawings are static, motionless, yet you manipulated the laws of reality and allowed them to animate and exist as they desired. You in essence became a god watching over his creation. This was the birth of your world. A world that you had sole control over. The world that couldn't be sustained as an adult.'

'I don't have a god complex.'

'I know. You just need control. The idea of being controlled scares you. You fear subservience or being perceived as such.'

'True.'

'So at a base level, this simple memory has had massive repercussions. Echoes. You forgot the Blib Blob because it out-grew your expectations. It consumed all you had created and as a result you left it to consume itself because you refused to give it anything more to feed upon. It died abandoned and you simply moved on to create something new.'

'I imagine that's what God has done to this world.'

'And in that sentence you've confirmed what I've just said. This innocent child shaped an adult concept.'

Daniel sits back in his chair, looks to the ceiling and sighs deeply. He lifts his hands and drags them down his face. 'There really isn't any hope for me is there?'

'There is, but it is going to take a lot of effort on your part. There is always hope.'

'Hope is so pathetically changeable.'

'So is life.'

Silence.

'So, Daniel, what now?'

'How do you mean?'

'Where do we go from here? Where does it lead us?'

'I don't know. Where does anything lead us?'

'I'm giving you control again.'

'But there was no control over that point.'

'I don't understand.'

'We moved the next day. All that was, ceased to be. Everything changed. I had no control.'

'So it was left behind? New start?'

'I guess so. The only thing that followed was the shadow.'

'What about your friends? Did you not think about them?'

'Never. Why would there have been any need to?'

'But they were your friends.'

'They were gone.'

'They still existed.'

'Not to me.'

'So, you were moved. Alone again. Restart, default. Clean slate.'

'I was four. What meaning would all that crap have?'

She leans forward. 'Change is an important part of our lives. Everyone we meet affects us. Your friends made a mark on you, and you chose to just forget them.'

'Who said it was a choice? It was just fact. An event. It happened. We don't choose for a film to end.'

'You do if you are writing it.'

'Fuck off.'

'Daniel.'

'Stop it. I don't understand what you're trying to do.' He rocks slowly in his chair. 'What do you want? A final memory with them? Okay, we drew a witch. She fell down the stairs and died. The page was a scribble of pencil marks at the end.'

'Who's "we"?'

'My friend obviously. That was the last thing we did together. We drew a picture.'

'That ended with death.'

'It ended with her death.'

'Who's idea was it that she fell?'

'Mine.'

'Why did she need to?'

'I don't know. The picture was drawn then I continued the story. I drew the scribbles as she fell down the stairs. I dictated her death. She died and then our parents picked us up.'

'You ended the friendship.'

'What?'

'Something in you knew that the scene needed an ending; that the friendship wasn't like the picture. It had no continuation. So you destroyed the last thing you did together. The story ended in death. Just like your friendship. Just like the Blib Blob. You created a conclusion. An end. *You* put the full stop at the end of the sentence.'

'I didn't kill anything.'

'You didn't harbour any feelings for those you were leaving behind.'

'I was four!'

'It was, *is*, your coping mechanism.'

He screams in frustration. 'It's life. Doors open, doors close.'

'In your world they close and lock. No going back.'

'It wasn't my choice.'

'The move wasn't. The emotions were.'

'So I've been a fuck up since birth?'

'No, you just like finality. Death.'

'Everything must die.'

She writes his response down in her notepad. She doesn't answer.

# FOUR

He looks at it lying there on the floor like a personified lie. He feels nothing. It's just a confirmation. A final piece shoved into the jigsaw that was so painful to put together but brings no satisfaction upon completion. How can it be denied? It wasn't there last time. It's there now. It all makes sense. The scratches on the back; the reluctance to remove the t-shirt. The little niggles at the back of his mind. The used and shitty condom staring smugly up at him. He may be crazy, but he's not stupid. All that will follow will be lies, a stream of bullshit that he is meant to believe. He doesn't care enough anymore to get angry or upset about it. He guesses something dies. He sighs inwardly. How sad, to be faced with so much hurt, pain and humiliation, and to simply be able to dismiss it under the phrase 'I'm used to it.' Just another notch on the ladder, another scar.

'It's not mine. I haven't fucked anyone else in this bed but you.' The lie.

'I didn't say you had. I just asked you why there was a condom on the floor.'

'It was probably from a while ago.'
'You moved into this room whilst I was with you.'
'It could have been my ex's. He stayed here.'
'It wasn't here last time.'
'Maybe you just didn't see it.'
'Maybe.'

The last time he had counted how many condoms had been in the box. A check on fact would prove everything. He opens the box and counts. Only four left. Some are missing. He can't remember how many there actually had been, but he knows it was more than four. Fact confirmed. Lie confirmed. He knows exactly who it was, well, has an idea of whom. He'd been expecting it anyway.

He showers, towels himself dry and sits on the bed, alone in his boyfriend's flat. Just him and the used condom. He can't cry. Not out of any form of pride, it just isn't emotionally possible. Blank. Just totally numb. Dead inside.

He walks to the kitchen. Rolls himself a cigarette. Click. Flame. Inhale. He tries for an emotion. Still there is nothing.

He is nothing.

He is worth nothing.

He is nothing.

Nothing but worthless dirt.

'Daniel?' Her voice is calm, concerned. 'Are you okay?'

'Sorry.' He's confused, dazed.

'You zoned out. Where did you go, Daniel?'

'Nowhere.'

'Are you sure?'

'I said "nowhere" didn't I?' he snaps.

She writes in her pad. 'What caused you to just dissociate?'

'Just something that was on my mind.'

'Did it replay?'

'It's none of your business.'

'Do you want to talk about it?'
'It's none of your fucking business.'
'Okay.' A pause. 'Would you like to continue?'
'If you want.'
'It is not up to me.'
'Then we'll continue.'
She sighs. Re-adjusts. 'So, you moved. Do you remember much of that?'
'No.'
'Was it important to you?'
'I didn't have an opinion on it either way.'
'Okay. So…'
'I remember my first day at the new school. I can see it now. As clear as you sat opposite me.'
'What happened?'
'I was fine. Stood next to my mum. Shown where I could hang my coat and bag. Taken to one side and introduced to the class. Then my mum tried to leave. I screamed. Clung onto her leg, crying, pleading not to be left alone. The teacher took my hand and pulled me away. She held onto me as I watched my mum leave. I hated her from that moment on.'
'Who did you hate? Your mum?'
'No, don't be stupid. I hated that bitch teacher.'
'She was doing her job.'
'She was a cunt.'
'Why did you not want your mum to leave?'
'I was scared, alone. Surrounded by all these new faces.'
'But you made friends with them?'
'A few.'

'The rest?'
'I didn't give a fuck about.'
'Even back then?'
'I had my friends, everyone else just existed.'
'Do you fear new beginnings?'
'Doesn't everyone?'
'Yes.'
'So what a redundant question.'
'You see, in situations like that…'
'Don't give me that crap. I was four. Most four year olds would have reacted the same.'
'True.'
'So don't label me out to be any different.'
'It stuck on your mind.'
'No, it didn't. It just came back when you asked about the move.'
'Yes, but…'
'Next question.'
'Daniel…'
'I said stop trying to find shit that isn't there.'
'You changed, Daniel what caused this anger? You have dissociated and now I am talking to your rage.'
'You're talking to me. I am one person.'
'But you see other versions of you in your head.'
'Yes, and?'
'Can you try and calm down please?'
'I…' He breaks off.
'What has upset you, Daniel?'
'I love him.' His eyes stare lost, misted.
'I know, Daniel.'
'I fucking love him.'

'We will get to that part soon. First we need to find a cause of what has happened in your past to make you act like this.'

'I love him.'

'I know.'

He cries. She sits back and lets him. There is nothing more she can do.

# FIVE

'Do you have problems trusting people, Daniel?'

'What?'

'Trust.'

'It's a wasted notion.'

'Is it?'

'Everyone hurts you in the end. Trust means nothing. Everyone is too good at lying these days.'

'How can you base any form of relationship if there is no trust?'

'Trust gets broken.'

'Daniel.'

'Even when there's an apology, that trust is gone if they can't answer the evidence in their face.'

'Maybe the evidence was wrong.'

'Okay, here's a scenario. There's four condoms in a box. The next time you check there's three and one empty packet. You ask. You get "I didn't fuck anyone." You ask how there comes to be one empty packet. They shrug and say they're going to bin the remaining condoms to "save you from having to count them." What does that say?'

'What if they are telling the truth?'

'So where did the other condom go?'

Silence.

'If they are the only one who has access to that box, where did that condom go? Someone is lying. It's not you because you counted the condoms.' He pauses. 'So, where does the trust lie in the situation?'

'That is a one off.'

'That's an example.'

'You cannot quantify trust like that.'

'Why not? That's the person who holds your heart in their hand. They could put your mind to rest by telling you where it went, even if that truth is painful. Instead they choose to deny it, a shrug of dismissal, the all-encompassing "I don't know." But they do know, they're the only one who had access to that fucking box. They choose to let you suffer in the visions and scenarios in your head. They choose to cause you extra pain through not knowing the truth. Why should you trust after that?'

'Daniel, that is just one experience.'

'People withhold truths in order to prevent hurting people. They lie and let the other live in ignorance because it's easier that way. How can you trust liars?'

'Can you trust me?'

'You're sat there judging me. I'm a patient. Your care is only for the fulfilment of your job. You don't care for me as a person. You're not my friend.'

'I care about you getting better.'

'That doesn't mean I can trust you. You're judging me on everything I say, trying to find ways to point it into a meaning or a delusion.'

'How long have you been incapable to trust?'

He shrugs. 'I can't remember. I try to trust but it always gets thrown back in my face. So now what's the point? Expect the worst, that way when it happens it can't hurt you as much as it could. Mankind is a genetic liar. History has proved that time and time again. What's the use of trust when no one truly values it? Lies save face;

they create truths for the teller's benefit. I've been hurt too many times to realise that you can have relationships and friendships based on no trust at all.'

'Do you not find that sad?'

'What?'

'To experience so much pain and upset and just shrug it off with "I'm used to it".'

'That's life.'

'Does not have to be.'

'That's my life. What's the other option? Ignorance? A lack of knowledge? Living in the dark, closed ears against the prison of reality? Everyone is out for something. You have a use. If you're just a commodity then what use is there believing otherwise?'

'The prison of reality? Reality is real, it is infinite. It is not a prison. Surely existing in your mind is a prison.'

'Reality is a prison. Life is the sentence. You all think that you're free but the reality is simple: you're not. To live you need money, for money you need to work. When you work you are in service to someone. That is not freedom.'

'We have free will.'

'Really? Can you turn up to work paralytic without consequence? Can you take recreational drugs legally? Can you fuck whoever you want regardless of their opinion on the matter? No. Your "free will" is defined by others. You are subservient therefore not free.'

'That applies to you as well.'

'I know, and I hate it. I despise your world. I don't want to be a part of it.'

'But you are.'

'Not by choice.'

'Okay, Daniel, I want to return to talking about you.'

He says nothing.

'Is that okay?'

'That's why we're here.'

'So, to move forward a bit, we have already spoken about the figure in the sky, is that the only time that that kind of hallucination has occurred?'

'Who said it was a hallucination?'

'People do not appear in clouds.'

'In your opinion. To me it was real.'

'Okay.'

'There was one other time I remember.'

'Age?'

'Ten.'

'Tell me about that experience.'

The rain falls. Giant, ceaseless drops of water pissing down from the heavens. It had been raining all night and all day. So much rain. He couldn't remember when he'd seen this amount. The lightning had followed. So did the thunder. Hand in hand they rolled across the sky. The perfect partners, together forever, the cause and effect.

The world looks grey. A dull monochrome. The water continues to pour.

\* \* \*

'I wish the world was lit as I see it. The colours so muted like watching old sixties home movies. Worn out. Faded. The last gasps of air on the wind tunnel of life.'

'Daniel, that was a quick change.'

'It's just an image of perfection in my head. I'm sat on the chair smoking, high on ketamine. The world is falling asleep as my computer plays Radiohead on random. I'm wearing blue jeans, ripped, faded. A white t-shirt. The sofa is old, tired. It's on the opposite side of the room to the computer and the window it sits next to. I could be anywhere. The scene is perfect. I'm alone and writing, locked in the moment. An imagined sun setting and I am alone with my music in my room. Technology and organic. I could be sat typing, but instead the computer just sings and I sit with a notebook on my lap, pen in one hand, cigarette in the other.'

'Why is it perfect, Daniel?'

'Because I could be anywhere. London. Miami. Rome. New York. I'm locked in the zone so the surroundings have no culture. I just exist. I feel at peace. I know I'll be here again. I'll always be able to return here.'

'What do you mean?'

'Here. This place in my head is where I want to exist. The place I see now. I am at peace. I'm creating. Doing what I do without interruption from the realities of your world. Good music, ketamine, a notebook, a pen, tobacco. That is Heaven.'

'Daniel, are you okay?'

'I just want to stay here.'

'Daniel, you are not making any sense.' She leans in and looks into his glazed eyes. 'Daniel, you have zoned out. Come back.' A click of her fingers. 'Daniel?'

He jumps. Sits up straight and looks at her. 'Sorry.'

'No, it is okay. Today has been a hard session, but I do not want you to go to that place just yet.'

'Where were we?'

'You were telling me about that moment in the rain when you were ten.'

'Oh, okay.'


The rain falls. Ceaselessly pissing down from the heavens. So much rain, it feels like it hasn't stopped for days. Heavy, thunder and lightning its bedfellows. The world outside a grey monochrome. He watches all this from the window. *Could you stop the rain from falling if you just asked?*

The clouds march forward, an army shedding its tears of regret. Never ending. A drop of infinity spilt upon a dying world. A constant cycle in motion. He pulls himself from his chair, and puts his hands against the window. 'I can stop this,' he says aloud. His friends turn. 'I can stop this,' he repeats adamantly.

'Prove it,' someone says. He doesn't know who; he's lost in the moment.

'I will stop this.' He walks away from the window and out of the classroom. He knows it will stop. He knows it. He pulls on his coat and walks from the school, walks to one end of the playing field. The ground churns to mud under his feet. He stops. In position. He eyes the other end of the field. *This will have an ending*, he says in his head. *This will stop before I reach the end.* He walks.

Eyes cast to the heavens he walks. Muttering constantly under his breath. 'What do you want? Show me a sign that you can hear. Make this stop. I command this to stop. Show me. Show me what you want.' The words flow. Constant. Never ending. His voice rising in volume.

Arguing against the howl of the wind. Arguing for dominance. His walk determined. Focused. He knows people are watching. He doesn't care. He has a task to do. 'Show me!' he screams. 'Show me!'

The world turns silent. The drops slow, they fall as light as a snowflake. He can see each unique drop twinkle like crystal before exploding against his frame. The air filled with a hum, dark, ebbing and flowing like waves on an ocean. The noise of the darkness entering his ears. The thunder breaks, he feels its vibration as the last electric blue of its lover fades from sight. He still walks, slowed by the scene. His eyes never leave the sky.

He sees the cloud crack, sees the line run across it before it peels back like the rind of a rotten fruit. There it stands within the cloud. Tall, gaunt, surrounded by tendrils of black smoke. Featureless it stares at him; stares deep into his soul. A vision in the grey clouds. They look deep into each other in silence. All sound muffles then fades to nothing. His feet stop moving and he just stands motionless as the crystal drops shatter around him, their explosions glorious. Beautiful. The whole moment lasts an eternity. Millions of atoms explode, create their universes, live, die, implode. Nothing.

The shadow explodes into millions of black flies; they dance erratically as they escape the sound of a thunderclap.

Then nothing.

The noise returns. The rain pisses down on the earth. Everything returns to how reality intends it. He shakes his head. Tries to escape the realisation that everything that once was will die in nothing, with nothing. He feels empty.

His eyes refocus. Above him the clouds are parting. The rain slowing to its end. The sunlight baths the sky with blue.

He turns to look towards the building. He can see silhouettes looking back at him. The rain stopped. He'd done it. He'd said he'd stop the rain and he did. *He* created the ending.

He still feels empty.

# CONVERSATION II

# SIX

'They're disgusting,' he says.

'Who are?'

'All of them. Each stinking, vile specimen of them.'

'Who?'

'Mankind. The whole of humanity is rotten. Dead inside. They are a cancer.'

'What has happened since we last met to make you feel this way?'

'It's always been this way. Always has and always will be.'

'You can't judge everyone, Daniel.'

'Yes I can. Each and every one I've met has been a deceitful liar. You place all that trust into them and they all fuck you over. They lie; they say what isn't true. There is no honesty.'

'But you are part of that race. Do you not do all of those?'

'I try to be honest, I try to tell those that matter the truth.' He pauses. 'I can see the lies in their eyes; they think they can hide it but it's there. It can't be denied. What sort of person can look you in the eye and say "I love you" when they have feelings for another?'

'Can you not love more than one person?'

'Maybe, but y'know, they think you're a dick, and that they're not happy with you. You know they would rather be single, that's what they tell others, but to you they lie, waiting for you to do something wrong so that you get the blame for the ending and they walk away the innocent party.'

'If you see all this and know that they may not feel the same for you, why do you stay? Why don't you be the one who takes control? You like being in control.'

'Because I love them, and that hurts even more. I love them and know it's not the same. I know one day they will leave me, but I don't want to be alone. I just don't want to be alone. I just want to be loved as much as I love them. I want love in this stupid reality of yours to be as real and as true as it is in my head. I want it to be more than a simple four letter word.'

'But love does exist.'

'Not for me. I'm not good enough. I never get it. I see everyone else in these "loving" relationships and I hate it. It makes me feel like dirt. What is so bad about me that means they can have all that and I can't? Then I think about how many lies each of them have told, how many sordid truths have been pushed to fester under the carpet. Then I think why bother?'

'Trust?'

'Trust is as pointless as love. You trust someone not to do something and there they are, doing it behind your back, then lying to your face. Then when it all comes out, what happens to that trust? It was meaningless. It was nothing but a lie.'

'We have already spoken about trust.'

'Then you should already know.'

'I was checking for consistency.'

'You were doing your job.'

She sighs. 'So, Daniel, let's talk about love.'

'What about it?'

'What does it mean to you?'

'Everything. *Everything*.' He pauses. Looks her in the eyes; she averts her gaze from his tears. She can't speak. He cries. 'Everything. I guess I loved them all in their own way; each of them stole something from me. Now I have nothing. I can give no more.'

'The heart has no limit to how much it can love.'

'But I do. I loved them all and they all did the same. I was never good enough for them. They wanted others. All planned my disposal before they had the guts to do it to my face. People knew before me and that hurts more than anything. The pain too much to word. What is wrong with me?'

'I cannot answer that.'

'I just want to be loved. I want it so much that it hurts. A constant pain. I give them everything, but it's not enough. How can I give more than I have?'

'No one should expect you to.'

'But they do. It always ends this way. Everything falls apart and I'm left of my own.'

'Tell me, Daniel, when was your first relationship?'

'What with? Boy? Girl?'

'Which ever you consider most important.'

'Twenty.'

'Okay, when did you lose your virginity?'

'Fifteen.'

'Is there a reason for the five year gap before you met someone?'

'No. There was no one I wanted. No one did it for me. It was simply about the sex.'

'So you cared about them?'

'No, it was sex. You don't have to care about who you're fucking.'

'Did you not care in the sense that you were giving them something they enjoyed?'

'It wasn't about them. I couldn't care less if they enjoyed it or not.'

'Did they ever show interest afterwards?'

'A few; most wanted to have it again.'

'And?'

'And what? As soon as they started to get too into me I'd throw them away.'

'But is that not what you said you do not like?'

He laughs. 'Are you comparing what I said about love to a meaningless fuck? I fucked them, that's all. Nothing more, nothing less.'

'You used them?'

'They're human. That's what they deserve.'

'But you hate being used. So why use someone?'

'They benefitted from it. Everyone enjoyed it.'

'Right.' She scribbles in her notebook.

'Is this about love or sex?'

'Both. Sex is important in both.'

'Love goes beyond sex.'

'Tell me about your boyfriends.'

'My first dumped me on holiday. The second wanted to fuck around, as did the third. The fourth break up was a misunderstanding. The fifth I cheated on. Sixth wanted to fuck around. The current... who knows, he already has.'

'I asked about your boyfriends, not their endings. You always talk of finality.'

'Everything ends in nothing. Whatever legacy we may leave will be tainted by others to their own means and will remain for only as long as it is remembered. Nothing is our destiny. We are born from it and to it we will return.'

'And love? Is that not eternal?'

'Not in this world. It dies.'

'Does your love die?'

'When there's nothing left to love, or when there's nothing left to hate.'

'I don't understand.'

'You can't have hate without love. There's always a point where there is nothing left to hate, but the question is: if love ends in hate, and hate dies, then what the fuck was there to love? Hate is true love's conclusion, and when there is nothing to hate there is nothing.'

'Love does not have to end in hate.'

'True love does. True love is meant to be forever. If it is lost there can only be hate in its place.'

'That is a very negative viewpoint.'

'That's truth. That's how it works.'

'In your world.'

'In any world, only yours can't support true love. It's too jaded, too rotten. Its core is dead.'

'Lost its meaning?'

'Exactly.'

'I do not agree.'

'You wouldn't.'

'So try and make me.'

'What would be the point? Everything I say you judge, label and pack away into a box. If it doesn't fit in exactly, you get a new box off the shelf, place a new label on it and pack it away in that. So what happens when you run out of boxes and labels? Then you lock us away and study us. That is how you work.'

'Do you believe that?'

'Isn't that what you're doing? Isn't that why I'm here? I think differently so therefore I'm wrong. I'm broken. I'm an error that you need to fix.'

'Do you need to be fixed?'

'According to you.'

She scribbles on her pad.

'See, you're doing it right now. Can't you just accept some people can see clearer than you? Can't you accept the fact that somehow our worlds are better than yours? We could make yours better.'

'We have already discussed this.'

'And you never answered.' He leans forward. 'Does it scare you? Imagine if you let the darkness in for one moment. Imagine seeing through my eyes.'

'Daniel, stop it.'

'Yes. Yes, you're scared.'

'We are not here to discuss this.' The force in her voice causes him to snap back against the chair. The smirk deleted from his face. She continues. 'Do you mind if we return to the point at hand? Your negativity towards love and emotions.'

'Okay.'

'So what do you think is the problem? Why do you think you are treated the way you are?'

'I'm different. You can tell people sense it. It's like they can sense the illness in me, just like other pack animals. You can see it in their eyes. You can just see it.'

He rocks slightly. 'I'm nothing special. I never have been. Always just average and awkward. Average looks, bad hair. Too skinny. I'm nothing that would draw attention. I have lived in the shadows with ease and they can sense it. They can somehow see the darkness around me. Be it fear or repulsion, they react to it, even though they may not know the reasons why.'

'And this conclusion is brought about because?'

'The way people look at me. You can see they think I'm different, even if I dress the same as everyone else. They have the look. They're judging me, mocking me for not being the same as everyone else.'

'So you feel isolated?'

'I'm always isolated. Only the shadows welcome me with open arms.'

'So tell me about your experiences with love.'

'I loved them all, I think. To different degrees.'

'I know. So tell me about the most recent.'

'He's the only person who has been able to stop me in my tracks at a glance. Y'know, caught my eye and bang, "Whoa fuck me". He was, *is*, beautiful. The guy I'd spent my whole life searching for and there he was, directly in front of me...'

The club is dark. He opens the door and walks over to the bar, his friend following behind in silence. He orders, pays and turns. The music blurs and he freezes. His eyes locked. Everyone else is a blur, featureless and unimportant. Lost to the beauty of one. The one stood a few tables away. For the first time in his life he knows this the one he has searched for. The one he should meet. A crossing of destined paths. One moment of meaning in a lifetime of nothing. He senses his friend talking to him. He ignores it for a few more seconds before tearing his eyes away.

'He's fucking hot,' he says.

'He's alright,' replies his friend. 'Nah, you're right, he is hot.'

Daniel smiles. 'Shame he's obviously on a date.'

'Like he'd want you.'

'Thanks.'

'He'd more likely go for me.'

'Cheers.'

He continues to stare. To make eye contact. He feels his friend wrap his arms around him like a boyfriend. 'What are you doing?' he asks.

'You're here with me.'

'So?'

'So stop fucking staring at him and pay me some attention.'


'Do you think your friend was jealous?'

'What?'

'Do you think your friend was jealous that you were paying more attention to this guy?'

'Maybe. Who knows?'

'I think you do.'

'Yeah, okay, maybe yes. We were fucking at that time, but it was just that: fucking.'

'Did he feel the same?'

'No. I think he liked me.'

'So why did you not focus on what was in front of you?'

'I didn't feel the same.'
'Did you tell him that?'
'In a way.'
'So you led him on?'
'No.'
'If you knew how he felt then why did you not say that you did not feel the same?'
'It wasn't my place to. I'd made it clear it would go nowhere.'
'Not clear enough evidently.'
'Why does it matter? He didn't connect with me on the level he wanted me to, that's not my fault. It's not my problem.'
'So then, do you think it was love at first sight for you and your to be boyfriend?'
'Did I say "love"? No, but when I first saw him it was like walking into a world where the type of person I wanted exists and for once was interested in me.'
'Destined?'
'Maybe.' He fidgets in his seat. 'Maybe luck. Most likely luck. A chance meeting.'
'Significant?'
'Totally. A beacon of hope in the dark.'
'So did you speak to him that night?'
'No. I couldn't bring myself to do so.'
'Why not?'
'I thought he was on a date. I thought he was taken.'
'It is lucky you met again.'
'Totally. When he messaged one of my profiles there was no way I was going to let him slip through my fingers

again. It was the universe working in my favour, for the first time things went my way.'

'Your first date?'

'We sat in the pub and drank. It was nice; we got to know each other really well. It was mutual agreement. We liked each other from the start. Well, that is what I told myself anyway.'

'You do not know?'

'Who knows anything for certain?'

'Valid point.'

'When it was time to leave, we kissed. He couldn't leave, and I didn't want him to go either. We lingered, kissed again then went to another pub. He stayed the night at mine.'

'Did you have sex?'

'No, we agreed we wouldn't fuck. Not until we were ready. We fooled around though. It was perfect. It was rough. A lot of scratching, biting. He spat in my face. It turned me on. It was the kinda sex I'd been looking for for ages and finally I'd found someone who could provide it.'

'Were you happy?'

'The happiest I'd been in ages. I missed him when he left the next morning. I was surprised he wanted to stick around.'

'Why's that?'

'He knew the next day I was having a psychopathy assessment for the treatment unit I was being sent to. Who would normally be so accepting of that? "Hello, yeah I'm being sent there for two years." Not the most appealing thing in the world is it?'

'How did that make you feel?'

'It made me feel good. It made me want him more. I didn't want to lose him even though we'd only just met.'

'How about your previous boyfriends, did they make you feel the same initially?'

'With the exception of one, no. But even against the others, this time it felt different. Felt more important. I thought no one would be able to love me again. I thought I'd never be able to love anyone else.'

'Why did you feel that way?'

'Fear. There's only so many times your heart can get broken before you give up. With each time someone stamps on it, they kill the desire to flow back into the situation again. You begin to fear love. You see it for the deception it truly is. Love is not the greatest emotion in the world; it only sets the scene for it. Sets everything up for its conclusion, the inevitable loss and the pain that accompanies it. Love is a liar.'

'But how can you deny yourself an emotion?'

'You can't. I said you fear it. You face every possible beginning with dread as you know that inevitably at some point love will set up home in your heart. The only way to avoid it is to run from anyone who tries to get close to you. To ensure you stand alone, you run.'

'Run to where?'

'Nowhere. You just run, without direction or conclusion. The only problem is I don't want to be alone. I don't want to walk through the dirt of existence all by myself. So I have to face it head on. I can't run anymore. I have to stare at oblivion with every decision I make in my life. You realise there is only one Hell, and that is *this*. This world, this ball of hate orbiting a dying sun is Hell.' He pauses, he smirks. 'I found love in Hell.'

# SEVEN

He stops, he can't move. He has no idea where he is. Everything looks alien to him. This shouldn't be happening, this shouldn't be the way it is. He clutches his phone in his hand, showing him a way home. A simple straight line but he can't connect the map to reality. Everything runs past him, people, cars, time. He just sits there. *Focus*. Life drops frames and everything is a jerky trip that can't focus. Blurred. Long ribbons of light trail behind everyone.

He slaps his head and tries to shake some sense into it. He can't just sit here doing nothing. He needs to get home, back to his sanctuary; needs four familiar walls to box reality into a prison that he can manage. He knows his other half is out having fun. Some bullshit about an unplanned meeting. He knows his lover wanted to go out, he'd mentioned it during the day but now the lie gradually becomes a truth and he's in no fit state to be part of it.

'Shit,' he says aloud. 'Fuck.'

He's fucked, completely on his own and with no one to turn to. He puts his earphones in to ground him. Play is pressed and the soundtrack doesn't fit the film. *Fuck*. He is actually panicking. Normally he would laugh at himself, but he knew it was going to be a bad trip from the start. Bang! Stop thinking about the past and deal with the now. He needs to get home. He needs to be safe.

*Focus. Fucking focus. Right.* He looks at the shops. They look different, everything curved in a giant fish-eye.

Ignore what you see. Follow what you know. His body kicks into autopilot. Trapped inside a robot he watches the nightmare speed by, tries not to pay any attention to it.

Faces, people, trees, posts. He walks. His head screams. He wants to run, cry, grab onto someone for help. Anyone. *Somebody help me! Anybody?* He is alone.

That clicks. The realisation locks and he understands why he has called no one. He is alone. He has to survive alone. People often give their sound bites about being there, always supporting, but it is bullshit. As he stumbles on, he knows that the reality is no one gives a fuck. They only care for themselves; they only look after number one. He knows his boyfriend is out enjoying himself, not giving him a second thought; he might even make out with a few strangers, that seems to be his thing lately, but the fact remains: whilst this hell is happening, no one is thinking about him. No one gives a fuck about him.

No one.

His key unlocks the front door; he slams it shut behind him and falls against it. He cries, sobs. He's alone. So alone. As his body rocks in anguish, the darkness wraps its arms around him. The shadow looks forward in silence.

'How is this relevant, Daniel?'

'What do you mean? Of course it's relevant.'

'We were talking about love.'

'Don't you get it? Love is irrelevant at the end of the day. You're always alone. Love is an inconvenience. An extra soul you're meant to think about as you struggle through Hell.'

She scribbles on her pad.

'All life is one sided. It exists from one viewpoint. It is selfish. You try to put all your effort into the one person you love and yet it is still *your* point of view and they still care about themselves more.'

'You do not know that, Daniel.'

'I know it from my perception, from my experience. At the end of the day we are all alone. All locked inside our own worlds. Everyone is so alone. That's the pain of humanity. To know. The knowledge. The knowledge that we can look into the eyes of the person we love and see the possibility that they don't love us in return.'

'But why would you look for that possibility?'

'You don't look for it. It just exists.'

'It exists through your fear.'

'Fear? I don't fear it.'

'Yes, Daniel, you seem to fear anyone getting a connection with you.'

'No, I fear looking into the eyes of the one I love and seeing only empty space. I fear that that one person can exist without me, without needing me. I fear that I will be replaced like a commodity.' He pauses. 'I fear being a commodity because then I'm just here for the taking.'

'Love.'

'What about it?'

'Do you think it exists?'

'Do I think love exists? Of course I think love exists. It sits right at the centre of me and governs what I do.'

'But you said you had a heart of darkness.'

'I still have a heart.'

'Okay.'

'I fucking love him, y'know.'

'Who?'

'My boyfriend. He means the world to me. I love him with all my heart, as much as is left open for use. But the biggest pain is knowing that he is fucking around behind my back. I love him. I love him and yet he could use the same language to say "I love it when you fuck me" to another. That hurts so much.'

'But that is mental pain, Daniel.'

'Mental pain hurts as much as physical pain. But unlike physical pain it lingers. It remains a part of who you are. It remains deep in your soul and is never forgotten.'

'Pain.'

'Pain is the feeling that keeps us alive.'

'Daniel, don't you see?'

'What?' he screams. 'What the fuck am I meant to see? What the fuck am I meant to understand? Just tell me what the fuck it is that you want me to know.'

'Daniel.' For a moment her professionalism leaves and she see him, sees him as the damaged soul discarded out into the gutter.

He cries, the tears fall and drown the sun. So much emotion poured out and sprayed across society. 'I love him,' he screams. 'I fucking love him.' The words resonate a form. A new wall built from the tears of the old.

'It is called comfort,' she adds.

'Hmm?'

'Comfort. You've created a comfort zone around you, a painful barrier that you control. You like to feel safe and anything that breaks that is expelled.'

'Comfort zone? You think this is "comfort"? Comfort is safe, it is peace, it is relaxation. This is Hell.'

'It keeps your world safe and at peace. It keeps order.'

'What the fuck would you know?'

'That you feel alone. That no matter what you do, you believe that loneliness is always your destiny. You fear connection because connection leads to loss, but at the same time you crave it as you don't want to be alone.' She sighs. 'So, what have we learnt today? That love is your everything, and despite everything you have experienced, despite you saying it is an inconvenience, you still believe in it. It is part of your life view, your world. In fact, I think it is part of its core.'

He rocks in silence.

'Let us look at your last memory. You said that despite the fact that you believe your boyfriend is cheating on you, you remain with him. The belief in your love for your boyfriend is so much more than your belief in his infidelity. Do you not think that is a positive?'

'Either that or I'm a fucking retard.'

'You can dismiss your staying with him as fear that if you leave him he will be free to sleep with the person you believe he is already sleeping with, but I see it as fear that if you leave him you will be losing love; maybe the most love you have felt for anyone.'

He snorts.

'Daniel, think about your other relationships, have you ever put up with as much as you have with the current?'

'No.'

'So what makes him so different? What makes him so special? Love.'

'I've loved in the past.'

'But you've let it go.'

'I've loved after I've been dumped.'

'You have obsessed because *you* didn't end it. It was not the conclusion you wanted. This is something different. You are trying to maintain control, trying to prevent a conclusion.'

'Fuck you,' he spits.

'Okay.' She pauses and sits back. 'Well, tell me what makes him so special.'

'I love him. I love him more than I have anyone.' He pauses. 'Well, I think I do.'

She snorts a laugh.

# EIGHT

'I remember them all.'

'Remember what, Daniel?'

'Remember when they all told me they loved me.'

'Tell me.'

'The first was in an email, it was the same day he told me he was HIV positive. The second blurted it out during sex, it was so unexpected that I had to stop fucking him. The third was hidden in a blog post. The fourth, we never said it. Fifth was at a gig, he told me and then ran away into the crowd. The sixth just blurted it out before we even got together and it stumped me to silence. The seventh, we were in a club, wasted on MDMA, it had a 'slut' in the club night's title; guess it summed it up perfectly.'

'Again, that was very matter of fact.'

'So? Why shouldn't it be? They are facts.'

'Did you tell them you loved them back?'

'Only to the seventh, the current. He is the only person where I've told them first.'

'So he is special?'

'I guess. He's something.'

'So, you wait to hear it first? To make sure you are not going to get rejected?'

'No, I wait until I know. I wait until I feel it. Love gives people too much power over you.'

'Power?'

'Yes, love is a form of control; it can be used as a form of torture, of punishment. Love makes people sadistic. Y'know, I sit and watch people treat those they say they love like shit. I see it in others; I see it in my own experiences. It's like they know they can push that boundary to its extreme because they know the other is so totally in love that they won't leave. They disrespect them, show no consideration for their feelings or their fears, all because they know love chains them together. I see all this and think what kind of world am I meant to exist in when something as pure as love can be used as such a cruel weapon. I see it in my own relationships. I see it and know that its presence means the grinding to an end and yet I struggle to keep hold of it for a reason I have no clue as to why.'

'Love.'

'Yeah. A four lettered word keeps me in a position where I am a joke, something they laugh about and go out of their way to make me look like an idiot.'

'They?'

'My boyfriend and his fuck buddy.'

'Do you know that as fact?'

'I've seen enough evidence to believe it, and he makes no effort to change that belief. I know where I stand in levels of importance.'

'And where is that?'

'Below the other guy. He is always more important than me.'

'Do you know that as fact?'

'I believe it to be fact.'

'Belief and truth are two separate things.'

'It is his job to make me believe different. He knows how I feel and he does everything he can to enforce that belief. He couldn't really give a shit about what I think. I'm not that important.'

'But that still does not answer the point that truth and belief are two different things.'

'What is truth? It's something that enough people believe in as correct. Science can quantify the truth through fact. On a personal level it is what someone wants to be true. A lie can become truth if enough people can be made to believe it.' He pauses. 'Pasts can be rewritten, recent actions reframed and redesigned. If no one saw the act then it can be removed, deleted and denied. When it comes down to it, what good is truth if you don't believe it to be its namesake?' He rocks slowly, his eyes filming over with tears. 'I could tell you a truth, a fact which most people would hardly believe, that most people would call it a lie. So what is the truth? The fact that actually happened to me or the "reality" the majority choose?'

'I'm confused, Daniel. Is there something you want to talk about?'

He nods.

'What is it?'

'I'm here because of love. That four-lettered word broke me. I'm here because of *him*, and no one would believe that possible because they believe him to be this big fucking saint. The blame was placed all on me and he escaped without fault. That hurts. How could I ever forgive that?'

'Who broke you?'

'The sixth.'

'How do you believe he broke you?'

'I don't believe it. I know it as a fact. A fact that no one would believe because they believe they know him better than the one person who had to live through it. This was the one person I put every thought into believing would make me feel the most worthwhile I've ever felt, and they treated me like the most worthless object in the entire world.'

'How so?'

'Don't you dare,' he shouts.

'Don't I dare what?'

'Don't you dare even trying to downplay this as a misinterpretation. Don't you fucking dare try to dismiss this as me not seeing the real picture. I lived through this each and every day. It was my inescapable life.'

'So tell me about it. That life.'

'It started out okay, perfect almost. It was born from an affair.' He smiles. 'That was always one of my fantasies, to fuck my boss, to have a work affair. I had it, then it became concrete. I chose him over my failing relationship. I followed what I felt in my heart.'

'You fell in love with someone you had not planned to?'

'None of it was planned. It just happened. I got caught up with it all, before I knew it we were in a passionate relationship, we used to fuck daily, at least twice, and it was possibly some of the most intense sex I'd had to that point.'

'Intense how?'

'Emotionally. It wasn't adventurous sex; it was pretty much vanilla but there was something there, a primal base.

I wanted to spit at him, smack him, punch him and bite his flesh, but that was not allowed.'

'Not allowed?'

'I don't think he would have got it, none of my exes ever have. None have allowed me to express myself sexually like that. So all the energy would explode in my head as a fantasy, so every time I came, in my mind I'd done so many unspeakable acts to him.'

'Did he know?'

'I couldn't care if he did or not. Anyway, that passion gave way to insecurity; my insecurity. He was so perfect in everyone's eyes that I felt so small, inadequate. Everyone always had such nice things to say about him and I've never heard anyone say anything close to that about me. I'd sit and just be quiet. I remember once someone saying to me "You're cute but your boyfriend, well, he's fucking hot." Although that was much later, but he still didn't care.'

'How did you live like that?'

'Who knows? Every day I woke up feeling crap, worthless, not good enough, and each day I would look to him to help fill those holes and he never did. He'd "try" but there was always some falsity in what he said.'

'Did you ever tell him how you felt?'

'Yes, I told him how I was uncomfortable with him being friends with his ex, about how perfect he was, about how insecure I felt around him.'

'How did he react?'

'He wrote me a letter; it told me to get over it, to deal with the fact he was friends with them. He told me he knew he was good looking and had a nice body. I was told to just accept it. What made it all so much worse was the fact that he believed it was okay for me be expected just to accept it, but when he had to deal with me meeting an ex for a drink he accused me of fucking him or still loving him. What was okay for him to do wasn't okay for me to do. Always one rule for him and another for me.'

'Did that annoy you?'

'Wouldn't it annoy you? I had all these expectations piled on me about what I could or should do and he had nothing. He was free to do as he chose.' He pauses. 'I lost all sense of self. I became withdrawn, someone else. Something I said I would never do. He is the only person who has made me cry about feeling so worthless… I can remember the day he killed part of me. His first fucking victory. I remember it…'

The sex had felt different. He'd simply gone through the motions as his mind ran through what had been said the day before, the cold harshness of it. It had been his birthday; they'd gone out for a meal. He'd paid for it. His own birthday meal flying out of his bank account; all £100 of it. His boyfriend had enjoyed it, then they'd got home. He'd asked his boyfriend to make a simple cup of tea. The answer had been simple. 'Look at the time; it's after midnight. It's not your birthday now. Make it yourself.'

He rolls out of the embrace of his boyfriend and looks at the wall. Trying to find a reason for that sudden coldness; he feels as empty as the sex they had just shared. He feels his boyfriend turn round; he waits for an arm to stretch over him, to pull him into an embrace. It doesn't come.

'You know what?' his boyfriend says. 'You should stop trying to live my life.'

'What?'

'You're never going to be me. It's like you've invaded my space. I see you every day, both at home and work. You've placed yourself in my friends' group. You're always there.'

'We live and work together, what do you expect? I work for your company.'

'Yeah, *my* company, you'd best remember that.'

He feels the walls of his world begin to crack. 'What? What's all this about?'

'This is about you trying to be me. You even started dressing like me.'

'But you told me that I couldn't wear any other brand of t-shirt as it is all about promotion of the company.'

'Yeah, I know.'

'So what am I meant to wear if I can't wear anything else?'

'You just have to deal with it.'

'I don't understand.'

'My friends are mine. Not yours. It pisses me off that they seem to like you more than me. I mean, they all showed up for your birthday drinks.'

'It was after work.'

'I don't care. It's all about you. That's all you care about. "I don't celebrate birthdays," you said.'

'I don't normally. This was the first year since I was sixteen that I celebrated it. It's the first time I've felt part of something, that people liked me enough to want to spend time with me.'

'It's my life and you've invaded it. You ruined my birthday, do you think you have the right to celebrate yours after that?'

'I was fucking depressed! I felt like crap. I tried to make it up to you. I bought a cake.'

'That crap cake? That rubbish little carrot cake?'

'I thought it cheered you up.'

'I hated it.'

'Oh.' His brain screams. Noise. So much noise. *What the hell is happening?*

'You don't want me. You want to be me. You want my life, my friends.'

He can't take it anymore. He pulls the covers from his body and naked crawls from the bed. At the door he turns to look at the shadow that is the 'love' of his life. 'I don't want to be you. I don't want your friends. For every one of them I have my own.'

'You tell yourself that. When do they ever come and see you? When do they ever want to be around you? Some "friends".'

He is out the room before the end of the sentence. He runs to the back door and escapes onto the balcony with his tobacco. Closes the door behind him and crumbles naked to the floor. He rolls himself a cigarette. It takes him longer than usual, his hands trembling uncontrollably from both his emotions and the chill of the February night air. Click. Flame. Inhale. One drag and he chokes on the smoke; his pain forcing it back out. He tries to scream but the sound dies in his throat and all that exits is a pathetic whine. He cries. For the first time ever he cries over a boyfriend tearing apart his existence with no care or remorse. Just a sledgehammer against the porcelain frame of his being.

He claws at his head. The noise so loud that it hurts. The voices so packed that there is no possible space for any more but still more hammer at the doors trying to get in. All that pressure. He punches his temples, trying to find an escape. It's hopeless. There is no escape. There is no exit. This is his prison. This is his reality. This is his life.

He stubs his cigarette out on his chest.

'Where did you go once you had calmed down?'

'I got back into bed.'

'Was he awake?'

'I think I woke him up.' He rubs his eyes. 'He put his arm around me and kissed my neck as though nothing had happened.'

'How did that make you feel?'

'I cried. I broke down and cried in the comfort of the one who had shattered me. As he held me tighter he asked me why I was crying. My reply was a mumbled "Why do you think?" He just squeezed me and said "You don't cry. Daniel never cries." That was it. I cried to the sound of him sleeping.'

'Did you speak about it the next day?'

'I left for work before he woke up. And no, it was never mentioned again. He acted as though it had never happened. The pretence of the happy couple continued without pause.'

'Why did you not leave?'

'How could I? I was trapped in a tenancy agreement. If I ran I would have lost everything. I would have had nothing. I would have been alone.'

She writes on her pad.

'He would go away every few weekends to visit his family. He would make a big deal out of how happy it made him feel. I once asked him how he thought it made me feel hearing it all the time, especially given the fact that I couldn't afford to go and see mine, and hadn't seen my mum for almost six months. He simply looked me in the face and spat "That isn't my problem is it? Why should I care? I'm not going to stop seeing mine just to make you feel better." I hadn't asked him not to, I'd just said I didn't like it rubbed in my face. He didn't speak to me for the rest of the day after that. I was punished for being upset about not being able to see my own mother. Who does that? What kind of a person does that? And yet he would tell me he loved me; that I was the one. He'd beat me down to tell me he cared for me.'

'I feel there is no closure here.'

'I don't understand.'

'You have not been able to move on from this because you have no understanding as to why it happened.'

'I have moved on.'

'In part, but there is still part of you that is open. Raw. You have moved on from him and have your new boyfriend, but these parts remain like open sores.'

'He cut me deeply.'

'How deep, Daniel?'

'He cut a line and slashed it across the face that is my life. He disfigured me. He took what I was and drew a nasty scar right across it. Most people damage you superficially, but he created a big fucking cut and it tainted everything. A massive open wound that cut right across the past, present and the future.' He rocks violently. 'No! He will not have my future. That belongs to another. I need to get him out of my head so there is space for Jake to grow.'

'Who is Jake?'

'My boyfriend.'

'That is the first time you have referred to someone by their name.'

'I know.'

'Why is that?'

'Because he means the world to me and I can't escape that.'

'So, let's go back to your sixth boyfriend.'

'Quite fitting isn't it?' He giggles.

'What is?'

'Well, y'know, he's the cunt. The bastard who broke me and he's number six.'

'Daniel, I still do not get it.'

'The first time we went out he killed a big part of me. Made me become this person who wasn't me. Pulled along like a puppet; a hollow shell. He killed me. He's the only person who has been able to kill a part of me.'

'Daniel calm down.' She places her hand on his knee. It's the first time they have touched other than a handshake. 'He did not kill you.' She smiles. 'You are here talking to me.'

'No, he killed who I was. He strangled my sense of self. He sat there and made me feel like shit because I became part of his life. He accused me of trying to steal his personality, but as he said all of that he sucked me dry of my own self-worth. My creativity dropped. I became a shell. He made me a cave.' He pauses, rubs his hands down his face. 'Do you know what he did to me on our anniversary?'

'What did he do, Daniel?'

He rocks slightly. 'He fucking killed me.'

# NINE

He wanders through the flat. The lights are off and he moves around in the darkness with the help of the absorbed light from the street. His boyfriend had said he was going for a drink. One drink. He still isn't home four hours later. He sits on the sofa and rips up the card he had made to commemorate the day. He wraps the pieces in an old newspaper and throws it in the bin. They will both die unnoticed.

The sound cuts through the flat. His phone saying it's received a message. He runs for it. 'Hey, we're in the Black Cap. We're planning on leaving soon. Is it okay if my friend stays?'

He throws the phone onto the bed in anger. The Black Cap? A pub that is little more than a fifteen minute walk away. He'd been fifteen minutes away all evening and hadn't even asked for him to go meet them. He picks up the phone. 'Yeah, that's okay. See you soon,' he types as a reply. 'Happy Anniversary by the way.' The afterthought is sent after the first and disappears onto a phone screen elsewhere.

*It's okay,* he thinks. *They're leaving now so I can get things ready for them.* In the kitchen he arranges three mugs, puts a teabag in all of them. He fills the kettle and waits. Smokes a cigarette outside on the balcony. Fifteen minutes pass. So does three more hours. With raw eyes he looks at the empty display on his phone's screen. 3:00am.

He curls up under the covers of the bed and hugs his pillow for comfort.

Noise. He hears the front door open and two figures tumbling in. He hears them make tea in the cups he'd prepared. He hears his boyfriend laugh over a writing competition form he'd left on the table of the living room. He doesn't move. He doesn't even open his eyes.

His boyfriend comes to bed. He undresses and pulls up against him, putting his arm around him. A sigh. He feels his boyfriend sit up and look over at his face. Checking to see if he is asleep. He keeps his eyes closed and tries hard not to give away the fact that he's faking. Warm in the knowledge that his boyfriend had checked. He smiles inwardly. It dies.

Spitting on his hand, his boyfriend pushes his cock into his ass. Pushes it in and grips him tightly. He fucks him. In, out; in, out. No consent, just expecting him to wake up 'naturally'. He cums inside. Pulls out and falls asleep without a single word.

He bites back the tears. He said he wouldn't cry again like the last time. His head is screaming. He wants to scream but it is so painful the only noise it would make is silence. Another bulldozer crashes through the wall. He regrets having told his boyfriend he had been raped when he was younger. Raped by the one guy at that time he had believed he could trust. That trust had crumbled to dust with each thrust in his un-consenting ass.

He regrets breaking his promise to himself. That he would tell no one about his most vulnerable moment. Then at that moment of regret a new voice cuts across all the noise in his head. 'It's okay,' it says tenderly, comforting.

'You weren't to know. You simply told the one person you believed you could trust. Happy anniversary.'

'I hated him after that. Well, not hated, I just knew how little I meant to him. Who could do that? What gave him the right to break me down so much, to take that one private memory and use it against me? I knew then that the only reason we remained together was the money he owed me.'

'Was it a lot?'

'It was the reason he still had his business. A few weeks later he went away for a weekend. The first thing he said to me when he got back was "It's not my fault you don't have a life." He *was* my life.'

'What did you do after he said that?'

'I got a life. I went out with a friend of my ex and in that one meeting I knew exactly what was what. I met someone who liked me for me. Probably the nicest person I've ever met. When we made out at the end of the night, it was the most perfect moment I could recall. I was so happy. I walked home with the biggest smile on my face. When I got in, my boyfriend jumped out of bed and shouted at me. I was too drunk to care. He went and slept on the sofa. I slept the most content I'd ever slept for months. The next day he got in from work and as I sat on the balcony smoking a cigarette, he walked in the kitchen behind me and simply said "This, whatever it is, is over." I just shrugged. I didn't turn or say anything. I just finished my cigarette. I was free. It was the nicest feeling in the world. It didn't stop him treating me like crap but in that one moment I smiled, I thought of the other guy who had entered my life.'

'What happened to him?'

'He got away. We remained friends but that notion of relationship never became an option. He has inspired me more than he knows.'

'How does that make you feel?'

'It's nice to know he's still around. It's nice to have someone who supports me just because they want to.' He smiles.

'Is that alien to you?'

'Yes, I've never had it before.'

'So what happened with your boyfriend now you had broken up?'

'I found a new flat. I kept it a secret from everyone. It was the only speck of light in the darkness. Each time he would make me feel like shit, I would smile internally as he didn't know about my escape plan. When the day arrived I didn't know if he'd be in. My mum drove me to the flat and I went and got the parking permit, I had no idea if he was going to be there or not. When I returned I was shaking so bad I couldn't even scratch off the details. My mum told me that singular moment had broken her heart. Seeing me living in so much fear of one person. I knew then that I had made the right decision. I cried when I left but that was not because I was leaving. It was because once I'd removed all my belongings, the flat still looked the same. You wouldn't have known I'd left. It was like I hadn't existed at all. I left no letter, no message or forwarding address. I just vanished. I ran. I ran for my life. It's the first time in my life that I've run from someone.'

'Did he leave you alone after?'

'He sent me cuntish messages but I cut all ties. It was stupid, for the first few weeks I'd start panicking at the time he used to get home from work. It took a lot for me to realise that I was now safe. The first thing I saw him write on one of those online profile things was: "Finally I get to sleep in my bed." I'd walked out of his life and that was all he could say on the matter. Fucking bastard.'

'Did you feel free?'

'I felt in control. I had my life back in my own hands and it felt so nice. I vowed then *never again*. The love had turned to hate and it was bliss.'

'So you could move on?'

'I did. I tried. Then he came back in my life and screwed it up again. Not content with doing it once he did it all again, and I let him. I let my stupid notion that I still loved him cloud my vision and he got his claws back in.'

'So he had not changed?'

'If anything he was worse. He made no attempt to disguise his put-downs. He ran around telling everyone we were trying again, but to me he would simply say "I don't want you." He used me for what he could. Once again he broke me, to the point that I ran crying from a pub. Crying so hard that I couldn't stop. He even sat across me whilst I was crying and told me that I meant nothing and then took me back to his flat and we fucked. All he did was fuck with my head and without care. Then when he'd had enough he threw me away again with nothing.'

'It seems you had met your match with him. He knew your weaknesses and used them to gain control. He outsmarted you.'

'He took my control like it meant nothing. I can't believe he had so much power over me.'

'This world is a big ocean, and there are some really nasty sharks out there. He was a shark, luckily for you not so much of one that you couldn't escape.'

'That's why I said it's funny he should be boyfriend number six. I escaped him once; that was the first six. He broke me a second time; that was the second six. And now I've got to a point where he totally has no control over me. I've evicted him from my life and mind for a third time. That's the third six. Three sixes. 666. The number of the Beast.'

'Do you believe he is like the Antichrist?'

'He's fooled everyone. They all think he is this nice, loving person when in fact his is an evil, vindictive, self-aggrandising prick. So yes, in that way he is. He's the destroyer of worlds. He destroyed mine, but like the Antichrist, he didn't win. He might have destroyed one world but I survived. I got to love again and actually be loved in return.' He smiles, the most beautiful smile she's seen from him. 'That's the first time something has had a happy ending.'

# CONVERSATION III

# TEN

'How is the drug usage going?'

'Erm…'

'It is okay; I am not here to judge you. Just to understand.'

'I don't think it's changed. No worse, no better. Up and down.'

'Do you take anything for these sessions?'

'Never.'

'Good. I would like to think I am talking to the "real" you.'

'You are. I do have some self-restraint.' He smiles at her.

'Are you comfortable talking about them?'

'I have nothing to hide. I'm not ashamed about using them.'

'Okay, that is what I want to touch on in this session.' She opens her pad onto a new page and dates it. 'Let us ease into this at a logical beginning. When did you first think about drugs?'

'I don't know. They've always kinda been a fascination. I can't pinpoint the moment. There's just something beautiful about a line of white powder on a surface.'

'Do you prefer to snort your drugs?'

'Yeah, obviously. It feels more satisfying that way.'

'Have you ever injected drugs?'

He squirms uncomfortably in his seat. 'I remember watching *Trainspotting* when I was thirteen and being turned on by it.'

'Turned on?'

'Yeah, Ewan McGregor was hot in that role. I remember always thinking "I want to look like that." He looked good; it was good wank material. It felt like I was looking at my future.'

'You wanted to be like the character?'

'Yeah. Renton. There was something about him that I wanted to be.'

'Did you try to be him?'

'No. I didn't want his life. I wanted his charisma. Y'know. I dunno, he kinda has a confidence about him. People liked him.'

'That is the point of the film.'

'No, but that can exist outside of it. I just wanted to be like him. He's a bit awkward as well.'

'Would you say it inspired you to use drugs?'

'No, but it was something that I felt was a possible outcome of my life. Like I *knew* I could end up in that hell.'

'Interesting.'

'It's like drugs were part of my destiny. Like they were meant to be a part of who I am.'

'Is that something you want to believe? A reason for your choice?'

'No, it's like they chose me. Like they've always had their kiss hidden in my head before I even felt it.'

'Their kiss? You have a very romanticised image of drugs.'

'They're my longest relationship. My closest lover. They've coursed through my bloodstream more times than anyone's cum.'

'Do you love them in return?'

'Yes.'

'You love drugs?'

'That is what I just said.'

'Do you think drugs have affected you?' She holds her hand up. 'No, let me change that. Why do you think you have such a relationship with drugs?'

'They help me. They silence your world.'

'Silence our world?'

'Yeah. They cut out all the noise and order your world tries to enforce on mine. They allow me to exist solely in my world.'

'They cut out reality?'

'There are those who use drugs to escape from the realities of existence, there are those who use to justify their existence, and then there are those who use in an attempt to find a reality for their existence and a reason for it.'

'Which of those are you?'

'I found my reality, now I search for its reason.'

'So the third.'

'Yes, I'm not running from the reality of existence because I've never existed in your reality to run from it. The drugs cut you out. They let me be myself, in my reality. In a way, when you take drugs you too are pulled into it.'

'Into your chaos?'

'Yes. A chaos *you* can escape. To us your world tries to force an order on that which cannot be ordered. There is only chaos.'

'It does not have to be that way.'

'Yes, yes it does. Without chaos, order will stagnate.'

'It does not have to be that way,' she repeats.

'It does,' he shouts. It bursts out of his mouth and cuts the air to silence. He rocks. 'It does,' he repeats, his voice softer.

'Okay, Daniel.' She makes notes on her pad. 'So where do you want us to take this session?'

'You said you wanted to know about my drug usage.'

'Yes, I know, but where do you want to start?'

'I first injected alcohol.'

'Pardon?'

'I first injected alcohol. Jack Daniels to be precise. It was easy. My brother used to work at a vets, he would bring home syringes and needles. At first I used to use them to cut myself, to draw intricate patterns. It was like art, a moment that fades. I used to fill the cap of one of those small bottles of JD and I'd snort the spirit right up my nose. When the needles were there, well, that was a new addition.'

'Did you hate injections?'

'Not then.'

'Okay.'

'I can remember it; well not the actual event, just the aftermath. The stupid aftermath. One simple mistake. I left the syringe in my mum's bathroom. I got home from school one day and she just pulled my shirt sleeve up and checked my arm.'

'Did she find anything?'

'No.'

'What was your reason for it being there?'

'I said I was popping spots.'

'Did you have any?'

'One or two I guess. She didn't say anything after it. Although from then on she'd randomly ask me to show her my arm. I never made the same mistake again.'

'So what had been the real reason for it being there?'

'I told you. I'd injected a bit of Jack Daniels.'

'How did it feel?'

'I can't remember. I remember it burned on entry. I was pretty drunk after.'

'Did you ever do it again?'

'A couple of times. I didn't really like it. I tried to teach myself to hate needles.'

'So, you created a fear which made it into a form of self-harm?'

'I guess you could say that.'

'So was that the first time you had injected?'

'First time I willingly did. There was one time when I was twelve, some guy in their final year jabbed me with one.'

'Did it have anything in it?'

'Yes, I got pretty wasted from it.'

'Do you know what it was?'

'Nope, but I remember it feeling like what I now know to be ketamine.'

'Was that a good feeling?'

'It was amazing.' He smirks. 'Made me want more.'

'So it made an impact?'

'It made everything feel so much more like the world inside my head.'

'Even then?'

'Yes, even then.'

'When did you actively take ketamine?'

'Not for a long while, a few years. I didn't know what it was then, but when it finally, eventually found its way up my nose it was like finding Heaven on this shit filled rock.'

'So I would be right in saying ketamine is your drug of choice?'

'Yes, that and heroin.'

'That makes sense.'

'Okay.'

She doesn't elaborate; she just makes notes. 'So what next? How did you get so involved in drugs?'

He saw it in the bag. He knew he wanted it. The bag had been left unattended in the classroom so he'd rummaged through it. He'd seen the baggy containing the white powder and his eyes lit up. He'd gone to check if anyone had been around and now, satisfied he is alone, he makes his move. It is transferred from one home to another – his back pocket. A smug grin and he exits the room. Calmly walks away from the scene and the act dissolves into history.

Cut to him, later, in his bedroom staring at his prize, and what a wonderful find. He doesn't know what it is. It could be anything. *Only one way to find out*, he thinks. A line is cut and snorted. He sits up, minutes later he feels amazing. He likes the feeling. He loves his life.

'So what was it?'

'Speed.'

'How old were you?'

'Fifteen.'

'Was this before you had injected the alcohol or after?'

'Before.'

'Okay.'

'I liked it. I used it in school one afternoon, well on a few occasions, and for the rest of the day I was bouncing off the walls.'

'And no one noticed?'

'I was usually hyper so they just assumed I was just more manic than usual. One time I ran down the street on the way home screaming "It's Friday!" at the top of my lungs. I laughed so hard that day my face ached for hours after.' He laughs at the memory. 'I even jumped in the road as the bus was coming shouting "Stop!" The driver told me off for that. I ignored him and ended up hitting some old lady in the face with my bag as I swung it off my shoulder. God, I was such a little fuckhead.'

'I am sure you were just a typical teenager.'

'No. I was fucked. Always disconnected from everything. I could muck around, not listen to a single word said, not do a single bit of work, and yet I'd always walk away with top grades. It was like this body just absorbed it all against my will.'

'I think you were just really intelligent.'

'I think you don't know me.'

'True. I can only base my opinion on what you have said, and that is the conclusion I have come to.'

'What? The boy who is so intelligent he gets completely wasted on drugs.'

'You are still alive. You still survive. It seems drugs have been part of your life for almost thirteen years and yet you have never formed any true addiction to them.'

'I once spent four months doing speed every fucking day as a base and then did other shit on top of it.'

'And then you stopped, I am guessing, once you realised a problem.'

'Yes.'

'Then you were not addicted to it. You stopped without help or withdrawal.'

'I did other drugs.'

'Daniel, I understand your need for drugs, for example the dissociative qualities of ketamine, but you are not physically dependent upon them. You can go periods without.'

'Ketamine doesn't dissociate, it makes everything feel real.'

'It makes reality feel more like how you perceive it to be in your mind. It helps bend the boundaries between your world and ours, so to speak.'

'It's how the world is meant to feel.'

'It is how *your* world is meant to feel.'

'It's how my world *does* feel.'

'Not all the time, that is why you experience the problem of not being able to connect, why nothing makes sense.'

'It helps others understand.'

'Does it?'

'It shows them a glimpse of Hell. They can feel the touch of the darkness upon their souls, a small insight into the madness. But they get to escape, they get to walk away; they get to return to normality. A bit of the dread of mortality might stain their minds, but all in all they remain the same.'

'And you?'

'The hell I see when I'm off my fucking nut is a hell of a lot nicer than the hell I see when I'm sober.'

# ELEVEN

He wants to kiss him. He knows that for definite. Maybe it's the amount of K they've consumed in grainy lines up their noses, maybe it's his aura; whatever it is, the glow around him is amazing. He just wants to reach over and touch him, pull him close and press his lips against his tender skin.

The conversation blurs around him, he hears every word but his attention is locked upon one person. Three on a bed snorting lines off a dead man's face. *God bless the lines of fate*, he thinks. To touch or not to touch? It's not a question of trying to rekindle the moment they'd previously experienced; it's a question of whether he should go for it with another person present. A private kiss is one thing but to do it in front of another, well that can be assumed as meaning more. Maybe it is the K, but he wants him so bad right now.

He guesses he should try and work out where things are going. He'd only wanted friendship but then this emotion popped up its troublesome head and things changed. He smiles to himself. *Fuck, he's hard to read, hard to see what's going on inside that head of his*. Subtle moments mean a lot in this case. Closed people can be a challenge, but what good is anything if there's no challenge?

He's been in this situation before. Miss an opportunity out of fear or just go with it? You either mess it all up or you don't. Everything works in twos, a positive or a negative. *That's life,* he guesses, *always circular, always filled with questions. We can only ever see it through one set of eyes, our own, and they're always that little bit jaded.*

Another three lines are cut. She snorts one, he snorts one, he snorts the last. The powder hoovered up via Her Majesty the Queen; it's like a two-fingered salute of 'fuck you!' *A moment.* When the Queen snorts her mountains of Peruvian, is she vain enough to filter it past her own currency? Snorts a line then rolls the fifty quid bill into a cigarette and kicks herself back against her throne…

Back to the scene. Him wanting to kiss this vision of beauty. The whole scene is beautiful; he wouldn't change a single moment. Not one. He used the snorting as an excuse to move closer. They're touching now, his hand placed against his back and he hasn't flinched away. *That's good right? God I'm rubbish at this sort of thing, I always mess it up.* Sit, chill, enjoy. He rubs his leg. It feels good.

*Life, funny little concept isn't it. All these differing people; ninety-nine point nine percent not even registering on our radars, never even speaking to us. Then you get those you care about, then there's that small, microscopic selection that leave you feeling confused at their sudden importance to you.*

He leans in for the kiss. The lips connect and the moment breathes life. They melt into each other, a movement shared. Falling deeper and deeper into each other. Intimacy without a solid connection. It's perfect; it feels like the first time. Their first public kiss had been in a bar, it was followed by the dramatic show they'd put on beneath Centre Point. That had been drunken; this, well this is a different feeling. Intense. Not emotionally, physically.

A camera flash. A moment caught on film. *The* moment. The moment he'd been waiting for. *Some things actually go your way sometimes.*

Reality returns. The speakers continue to sing. You can put music to any visuals; build a soundtrack for your life's movie. Moments marked by noise.

Another three lines get snorted off the dead man's face. It's like the moment never happened, but everything we do leaves a scar, each word leaves a tear, each thought lingers. The K kicks in completely and directs the rest of the shot.

Unplanned and without thinking their lips meet again. Melting once again into each other as a galaxy of crystalline shards glistens across the bed sheets. *Do you actually breathe when you kiss? I can't remember. It's not relevant.* Ketamine removes the thoughts as all three of them, connected in different ways, evaporate off the planet together.

'That is one of the most precious moments in my life,' he says. 'It was the whole scene, how it felt. It felt more real than anything as it seemed to happen within my world. Like for once it was governed by my boundaries and that made it so fucking perfect.'

'Does the fact it is a drug memory make it any more important?'

'Not at all. All the K did was shut out your reality and let me experience something completely meaningful in a place I could connect to as a whole entity.'

'And who was the other guy?'

'The one that made me see that the relationship with number six was completely over.'

'The one you mentioned previously?'

'Yes.'

'Name?'

'He'll know, but I'm not having it or what we shared cheapened by your mind through an association to a name. As it stands this is just an incomplete image in your head. A name would cement it into a solid form which you can then dismember at will.'

'I just want to understand.'

'You want to analyse.'

'So, one of your most important memories is drug based.'

'Yes, but you must not forget that the drugs weren't the basis of it all. It was the emotions; the things that will remain after the chemicals have worn off. That's what you need to understand about all this. It has never been about drugs. They've just been a part of it. As innocent as a cigarette in an old fashioned movie.'

'What happened after?'

'Nothing became of it. We remained friends. Only friends. That's the way it runs.'

'What runs?'

'This life. It just rolls on and on, and I am left behind. It gets scripted around me. A moment of happiness, everything building up to a positive then it all gets snatched away. Always that one glimmer of hope and then that candle is extinguished.'

'Do you think that you influence it at all?'

'I am just a pawn. Controlled by an unseen hand. Always living for these conclusions to have them pulled away from me. Shown the sight of happiness but never allowed to experience it. Happy endings are not for me. That's what it keeps showing me.'

'Who keeps showing you?'

'The darkness. It shows me how things could be. How things should work out, and I believe it. Hold on to those images as if they hold some salvation. But that can't exist in this world. It doesn't. That isn't the way of mankind. That is why it must be destroyed.'

'I do not follow.'

'If I could live the life I see in my head, as it pans out, the beauty of it all, I would be the happiest person in the entire world. But that's it, I'm not happy. I'm not happy because the reality of the situation is so impossible that it can't exist. That purity touches your world and it dissolves into dust. It becomes nothing. That is what all of this boils down to; the root of it all. Nothing. Once that is in your soul you see. You see everything as it truly is. There is nothing. Nothing. Nothing. Nothing. Nothing.'

'But we exist, that is something.'

'There is nothing. Absolutely fucking nothing. It's all fiction. It's all a dream. We are all alone. We are all alone in this void of nothing. We might as well simply not be here.'

'That is a very pessimistic outlook.'

'It's the truth.'

'According to whom?'

'The darkness.'

'What is this darkness?'

'It's the nothing from which we are all born, and into which we all die.' He rocks slowly. 'For those souls lucky enough to be reborn, the tunnel of light they see at the end, is the opening light they'll see from their mother's cunt.'

She cringes at his language. 'And if a soul is not so lucky?'

'Then it will be shat out into the void to rot.'

'I thought you said the darkness was here to destroy, why would it allow any soul to be reborn?'

'It needs to enter into this world, needs to bleed through the cracks and seep into mankind's souls. Corrupting from within; eating away at the individual's light like cancer. Change cannot be rushed, it is a slow progress but when it happens it will be quick like revolution. I've heard the scream of humanity, it burns like the fires of Hell.'

'Did the darkness show you this?'

'Yes.'

'Tell me, Daniel. You said that when you first saw the darkness, it was trying to show you your soul. That it was somehow part of you. That you believed that you had a "heart of darkness".'

'I saw a darkness mirrored in me. Not because I created the darkness, but because the darkness created me. We are one and the same. I don't belong here; *this* isn't my world. All my life I've been screaming at your reality. Screaming from within a body that is not mine.'

'So you feel disconnected from your body?'

'Not disconnected. A prisoner forced to exist within this frame of skin and bone. The darkness plucked me from the void and held me in wait. Then a child was born without a soul and I was placed within it. From within this form I have watched that child grow and age. I have controlled it like you would a stolen car or machine.

'I interact with your world because it is required for me to do so. It is required for me to achieve what I was put here to do.'

'And that requirement is to aid this darkness?'

'It is to allow the darkness to enter into this world, to enter and corrupt the minds of the few.'

'Why only the few?'

'To change the minds of many, you need only change those of the few. Make them believe and they will take that belief to others to whom you have no reach. The message will spread like a virus and once it grows too big, too engrained in people's hearts and souls, then the darkness can topple it with the ease of a gentle breeze against a house of cards.'

'So the aim is to build up and then destroy what was created?'

'Isn't that the aim of every belief and ideology? Isn't that the way of mankind? All empires are built and destroyed by the same people.'

'Not always.'

'A ruler builds upon the past, but they do build and most, if not all, fall because they destroy what they had been part of building.'

'Do you destroy what you build?'

'Always, that is what is expected. I don't aim to do it, but the conclusion is always the same.'

'To take this back to what we started this session discussing, do you feel that your drug usage has led to this belief, that you have learnt this viewpoint through experiences which have not been experienced in a real manner?'

'No. As I said, the drugs numb the noise of your reality. I do not use them to escape but to be at peace in the world that mirrors my world. It makes all of this liveable.'

'How would you feel if I said I thought you may be dependent on them?'

'I'd say that you are finding an excuse as earlier you said you believed that I wasn't. I can exist without them; I have gone years without their touch. Yes, they do help, but no, I am not dependent upon that help.'

'Okay.' She makes a note on her notepad.

'You can write that I "denied" dependence, but that makes you the liar. I have told the truth. I have said "no", there was no denial there.'

'What makes you think I wrote "denies"?'

'I know.'

'But how can you know what you have not seen?'

'What did you write then?'

'It does not matter.'

'Then I won't continue to talk until I know.'

She sighs. 'I wrote: "he denies".'

'Told you. So you're in control of my care and yet you just lied so that I fit into your idea of what I do. You are a liar.'

'I did not lie, it is a formality.'

'That because I'm "crazy" I am unaware of what I say? That I am the liar for telling you the truth of my head?'

'This is not relevant, Daniel.'

'No, you're right. You know best. I'm the liar.'

'Daniel.'

'You're a bitch.'

'Daniel, I won't stand for that language.'

'You're a blind mindless sheep, following through textbook teachings to the letter because that was what you were told to do. One person wrote the "fact" that you follow and it grew in strength because enough people believed in it and now you call it fact. I think that illustrates perfectly the point I was making.'

She doesn't respond.

# TWELVE

'So, where do we go from here, Daniel?'

He shrugs.

'Do you feel comfortable with me continuing as your psychiatrist?'

'What's the alternative? My case being handed over to a complete stranger? Having to build a new relationship with someone who is going to approach me in exactly the same way. Is that what the other option is?'

'In a manner of speaking.'

'In that case, I'll stick with what I know. It took you long enough to drag me to this point, I certainly don't want to have to go through all that shit again.' He looks her square in the eyes. 'So, what are we waiting for? What do you want to see me deny next?'

'Daniel, we cannot continue whilst you are in this mood.'

'I know. I was joking. Let's continue as though nothing happened. It'll work best that way.'

'I understand that you feel that our trust has been broken.'

'I don't think, I know.'

'But you have always understood I have a professional obligation.'

'You're just doing your job. I understand.'

'Okay.'

'So…'

'So?'

'What do you want to talk about now? Where do you want to take this session?'

'Shall we stay on the subject of drugs?'

'If you want. I'm happy with that.'

'Okay.' She turns the page of her notepad. 'Putting the idea of drugs as an influence on your world; how do they fit in with the everyday existence of your life?'

'I don't understand.'

'Instead of acting as an escape, how do they fit in with how you live?'

'I told you. They're just a side-line; just like alcohol or cigarettes. They're my choice above drink.'

'But have they caused certain friends' groups to form?'

'Oh definitely. I agree that a lot of my friends have been "druggies", but it wasn't the drugs that brought us together, it was an understanding. I think drug users understand those of us who you'd say have serious "mental health problems". I think they've seen our world so they get it and are more accepting. Granted some of these relationships are healthier than others.'

'Well, that is just like any kind of relationship.'

'True. I've been disgusted by my own friendships when I've had the ability to compare them with other ones I'd made in their absence.'

'Care to provide an example?'

The night had been nice. Filled with conversation and copious amounts of ketamine. The conversation had been good; not shallow fables but deep interesting conversations based on genuine interest in him and the work he produced. He'd never felt so much a part of a conversation before and it had sat warm in his heart. The simple life affirming fact that what he did mattered, even if that was only to a few people, it meant the world to him.

They had ended up walking into the club at half five in the in the morning, but within ten minutes of their entry he had received the phone call from his friend pleading him to go be by her side. She was pregnant, or so she claimed. 'Distraught' was the word that crossed his mind. That was why both he and his boyfriend had struggled to find the correct bus through their drug-fuzzed brains. He'd rolled on in autopilot, just muttering the bus number they needed. He'd felt so helpless, stressed. Panicked. All of these events and contradicting emotions are the reason why they now find themselves sat in silence on a bus heading towards Camden Town.

The scene is lit like an eighties film. Muted colours, a bluish grey. Everything feeling new yet experienced. Two punks straight out of a gritty British film stumbling down the road into an unknown situation. A quick walk with minimal conversation. He knows what is coming and the 'oh you brought him' welcome they receive is merely a confirmation of that thought.

The flat they walk into is a mess, like a small bomb has exploded its belongings into unruly piles, discarded and unkempt out of disinterest. He'd been in there a few days earlier and it had been nowhere near as chaotic. The scenery matches the scene perfectly as though designed by an award winning set designer.

'Look,' she says, thrusting a used pregnancy test under his nose. 'I'm pregnant, Daniel, fucking pregnant.'

She's drunk beyond comprehension, her other hand grips onto the beer can she raises to her lips and swigs deeply from. 'What the fuck am I meant to do? There's a fucking parasite growing inside of me.'

His reaction comes too easily, warranting a shocked glare from his boyfriend. 'Get out a knitting needle and abort it then.'

They take a seat and she jumps onto his lap, opening her legs. 'It's right up there. Growing.'

'Do you want me to fist it out of you?' He smirks. 'I could punch you in the stomach, force it to bleed out.'

'Do it. Did you bring alcohol? I want to poison it before it has chance to breathe.'

'Do you know who the father is?'

'Yes, some French guy I fucked.'

'Should of bagged his cock with a condom. Was it a big cock?'

'Oh my God, it was amazing. How could good fucking sex give me this?'

'Could have been so much worse.'

'How could it be worse than this?'

'You could've got pregnant and got HIV.'

'You're meant to be comforting me, Daniel.'

'I don't know what to say other than get it sucked out.'

She falls silent for a moment, then turns to his boyfriend. 'I wasn't expecting you to bring him.'

'We were out, I couldn't leave him alone,' Daniel says mutely.

'Well, I don't like you,' she spits at his boyfriend. 'I think you're a fucking prick. Stupidly Daniel thinks you're worth it so I guess I'll have to accept his decision. End of the day, Daniel hasn't been the best boyfriend either.'

'Shut up,' Daniel says. 'Just leave it.'

'So.' She drunkenly raises her hand. 'Let's start again. Well not again because I don't trust you.'

'Have you done a second test?' Daniel changes the subject.

'What's the point?'

'Just do one to make sure.'

She scrabbles to her feet, grabs the second pregnancy test and leaves for the bathroom.

'She's a fucking mess,' his boyfriend spits. 'A cheap trashy whore.'

'We won't stay for long.'

'I don't want her empty friendship.'

'I know. Just humour her.'

A moan comes from the bathroom, the door flings open and she re-emerges into the room. 'Look. It's the same result.' Another test is thrust into his face. 'Not just "maybe", it's a "definite". There's some creature growing inside of me. What am I going to do?'

'Get an abortion.'

'Why did this happen to me?'

'You didn't use protection.'

'I asked you here to support me, not judge me.'

'I'm not judging you. I just said that's how it happened.'

'I can't believe it, Daniel, I could be a mum.'

'Do you want to be a mum?'

'It would be a sexy kid if I was.'

'Was he hot then?'

'Gorgeous.'
'Keep it.'
'I don't want it.'
'Abort it.'
'You're not helping.'
'What do you want me to do?'
'I'm too young to be a parent.'
'It would be an addict baby.'
'Imagine.'
'I don't want to. Get it hoovered.'

'Did she get an abortion?'
'Yes.'
'How did you feel about it?'
'What was there to feel? It wasn't mine. It was just an event.'
'So you didn't care?'
'Nope. It was just one of those things. Those moments that get consigned to a chaotic memory, laughed about a few weeks later.'
'Is it really something that should be laughed about?'
'Why not? Or should I hold some moral pro-life judgment? She got fucked, got pregnant, got rid of it. It's a simple series of events. It filled up about a week of her life.'
'Some people may say otherwise.'
'It doesn't concern anyone other than those involved.'
'What did your boyfriend think?'
'He thought the whole situation was disgusting. That she was a dirty slut that couldn't keep her legs closed. That I deserved better friends than those.'

'How did you feel?'

'Embarrassed.'

'Why embarrassed?'

'We'd had such a nice evening with his friends and then he had to meet mine. There was a stark difference between them. Like going from a nice restaurant to eat dessert in a rat infested gutter.'

'Are you being harsh on your friend?'

'No, that was exactly how it felt. I cried afterwards. It was like I'd had the sort of evening I've desired all my life with people who actually cared about what I did, then woke up and realised that it was a dream and the nightmare was exactly where I belonged.'

'Do you believe that is where you belong?'

'Yes.'

'Why?'

'I belong in the gutter, that is the life that has been chosen for me.'

'Chosen for you?'

'Everything in my life has been out of my control. Events have happened because I was guided in that direction and no matter how hard I've tried in the past to break free, all those roads have been blocked and I end up back in the gutter again. I am dirt. Worthless dirt. Worthless dirt belongs in the gutter with all the other trash.'

'So that is the life you chose?'

'I just told you; I didn't choose it. It was chosen for me.'

'By whom? Who chose it for you?'

'The darkness. I am its puppet and it has been playing master all my life. Controlling everything, leading me into the scenarios where its point would be made. I was born to experience the shit and loneliness of existence, the pain of not being included. The big machine rolls on and I'm left to exist in its tread marks.'

'You have the ability to change that. We all do.'

'No I don't. I have tried and with each attempt I have failed. Time and time again I have failed. The only path that I am allowed to follow is writing.'

'If you love writing, how can that be a negative?'

'I'm only allowed to word what the darkness commands. It pours its words into my head and I transcribe them into reality. If I try to write anything different then I can't, my mind empties and not even the simplest sentence will appear on paper. I can only write what is instructed; at the end of the day I am a fraud, taking responsibility for the darkness' work.'

'Do you not see that you must be writing from your unconscious mind; that you have disconnected the two so greatly that they appear to you as two separate entities? This might be due to no one praising your talent, it might be because you have such low self-belief and confidence, but they both come from the same place.'

'They come from the heart of darkness.'

'They come from you.'

'I am nothing but what the darkness commands.'

She sighs and makes some notes on her pad. 'Daniel, can I ask you something? Do you believe that? Truly believe it?'

'I believe it as much as I believe the sky is blue. It is my life, it has always been this way.'

'Have you always heard the voices?'

'They started when I was thirteen.'

'Did you never think of telling anyone about them?'

'No, they told me not to, that everyone heard them.'

'Daniel, I am at a loss. You have such a vivid imaginative internal world that has supported your existence, but that is it, it is just a fantasy; it isn't real. You learnt this existence and you're fighting so hard to maintain it.'

'Learnt it? How the fuck could I have learnt it? I'm not God; I can't create worlds of such vividness. What do you want me to say? That I see your point, even though I believe that you are lying? You are just trying to fit me into one of your perfectly constructed boxes so that you can stick a label onto me and file me away as "case solved". I have had to live with this all my life, had to be a prisoner inside a body that isn't my own. Who are you to offer an explanation?'

'But you wanted our help.'

'I didn't come to you; I was dragged here. You promised me that things could be better. You supplied the stupid belief that it didn't have to have been this way had I got help earlier. Do you know how painful that is? Everything could have been different, better, happier, or so you say. You have taken my life and turned it into a fiction, a badly written one. What gives you that right to play God over my existence? Telling me that I created all this. Are you fucking serious? Who would create a world like this? Who would create a world like yours? I have not chosen anything. The darkness controls me, and now you are trying to do the same. I am nothing. When it all breaks down, who the fuck am I? Am I what my life has created, or am I what you want to create?'

'You are who you want to be.'

'Are you not listening to me? I have told you again and again and yet you act as though I am lying, choosing deceit. Do you think that by saying a few select words you will flick a switch in my head and I'll be enlightened? And if so, why do you treat the darkness' mission for me as such an alien concept? Are they not the same thing? I want to flick the switch in your heads and open your eyes to your true reality; maybe that's what you fear. So lost in your own convictions that you fear that you could all be wrong.'

'Daniel, try to think logically.'

'What? Think by your logic? What if I'm right? I believe everything I have seen and I pray that I could see the look on your faces when you finally see the truth.'

'What is the truth?'

'You are the blind leading the blind. All that is needed is a shepherd to herd you to oblivion.'

'It is a fantasy world you have created.'

'What makes you so fucking certain? Is it those textbooks you cling onto as tightly as any bible or Quran? You dare to sit there and tell me my life is a fake because you didn't have the misfortune to experience it. What do we know about anyone? What we know about anyone is all based on the testimony of the person. What makes me different from anyone else? For all I know your entire life could be a lie that you have turned into truth. That's the same for every fucking individual on this planet. People existing in the lies they have made into a real life story, and yet here I am telling you the truth and you call it a lie. We know nothing about anyone; take my boyfriend for example. I have been with him for a year and I only know what he wants to be the truth of his time with me. So many secrets and lies, but they are covered over to the point that I don't even know who the fuck he really is. You think you know someone and then one thing tumbles out and in one painful moment you realise that person is not who you thought, and then their past actions invade your present and the distance is extended. The mask is pulled from their face and the truth is revealed. That is exactly what is going to happen to all of you. The truth will always come out no matter how deep you bury it. I live by the truth and I will destroy you and your lie built existences, then I'll watch as the shame of reality eats away at you until you turn to dust and the darkness finally fills your deceitful souls.'

'You are filled with so much anger and rage, Daniel. You have been hurt by too many people, so continuously it seems, that you have lost the ability to trust. You judge people by that belief and you lock them out on the chance that they might not be who they are. There are a great deal of people in this world who are honest and truthful that you taint with the brush of a few.'

'Everyone lies. Everyone has proven to live by the rules of deceit. Everyone I have ever known has been the same: users, liars. Everyone lets me down at some point.'

'I'm sure you have let people down.'

'Of course, this body is human, this mind forced to be human. But at least any disappointment I have caused has been from me just being myself. Being true to my life. Not because I've lived an existence that has crumbled around me.'

'Daniel, you are such a good person, so loving and creative; you could help so many people but instead you crave destruction. The saddest part is that you are so lost in your internal loneliness to see any of that.'

He cries.

'Why are you crying? Have I hit upon a truth?'

'No.' He breathes in deeply and wipes his face clean, erasing the lines of emotion. 'I'm crying because I know everything you just said was a lie. A beautiful lie, but a lie nonetheless.'

'Why was it a lie?'

'Because I am nothing. I am worth nothing. I am not lost in an internal world. I cannot help anyone. I am a prisoner in your world and my freedom will only be granted upon destruction.'

'Daniel, stop this. You are so much more than you believe, than you give credit for.'

'I am nothing,' he shouts. 'I am nothing more than a sum of the pain this existence forces me to feel. Don't you understand? I don't want to be here. I'm tired. So fucking tired but I am forced to continue. Forced to exist day after day when all I dream for is freedom. I'm tired. Just so fucking tired. I can't go on. I've had enough. So much pain. My soul stands naked in a stolen body and it feels each upset upon it like a raw and open wound because it has no body to call its own to shield it like you all have the fucking luxury of having.' He pulls his knees up onto his chair and hugs them tightly, burying his head into them. He rocks.

'Daniel?'

He looks her in the eyes. 'I don't want to be here anymore. I want to vanish into the eternal silence. I wish I could die, but to die I would need to be alive. This living machine.' He points at his body. 'Is dead inside.'

# CONVERSATION IV

# THIRTEEN

'You seem to always be in this situation, Daniel.'

'I know. Fucking stupid isn't it? And even I don't know why the hell I put up with it.'

'You must know.'

He shrugs, dismissing the presumption away with a simple body movement. He doesn't know what to feel. 'I guess it's like I said last time: a certification of it being right. You never truly know anyone.'

'What happened exactly?'

'He did it again.'

'Your boyfriend?'

'Yes.'

'Did he admit to doing it?'

'It came out the day after our anniversary. He did his usual underplaying and then bang. Truth comes out, always does.'

'What caused it to come out?'

'I asked if I had anything to fear about going for my STI tests. I guess he was scared he could have given something to me. I don't believe he would have ever told me otherwise. Part of me thinks that had I not asked, had my results come back in any way positive he would have accused me and used it as an excuse to run.'

'Is that not a bit of a harsh opinion to have?'

'Kinda. I only said it was part of me that thinks that. How could he have put me at risk? Am I worth that little? I mean I'm obviously not good enough.'

'Did he say why he did it?'

'He said he was wasted and got caught up in the moment. I believe he did it for the simple fact that he could, for the excitement of it all, and because the guy was leaving the country that night he didn't feel bad about doing it, as there was no chance I could bump into him. That's why he didn't tell me, nor was he going to. He thought he got away with it, just another secret to add to the pile. Shame truth said otherwise.'

'Would you have preferred not to have known?'

'I knew the moment I saw him after the event. I knew it, even asked him to his face. He lied and made me feel like shit for asking. I'm not stupid.'

'Did you talk about it?'

'It doesn't need talking about. I said on our anniversary that all the shit from the previous year would be past and we would start afresh. I'm more annoyed at the fact I'd given him a chance to be completely honest and he chose to lie. This could have been sorted earlier and without such issues.'

'Can you start again?'

'As it stands I don't feel I know who he is, so I'll have to relearn that, but he has to put in all the effort, I've put in enough for no reward.'

'Do you think it will all work out?'

'At this precise moment I don't know. I truly don't know. I got over all the other times he messaged guys; I got over the first time he did it. So I guess I'll get over this. Only now I'm thinking how many others there has been that he's chosen not to tell me about.'

'Do you think there could have been more?'

'I truly don't know.' He rubs his hands down his face. 'Can we not talk about this? It's only going to upset and confuse me more.'

'Okay, if that is what you want.'

'It is.'

'Can we talk about the shadow? We haven't spoken about it in a while and I think we are now at a good point to do so. Are you comfortable with that?'

He nods.

'Great.' A pause. 'What do you think it is?'

'I've told you. It is part of the darkness. It is my prison guard. It is here to make sure I complete what is expected of me.'

'And that is to transcribe the words this darkness puts into your head?'

'Yes.'

'We've spoken before about your earliest experiences with it. Has it always been a constant?'

'It's always been there. Biding its time.'

'Biding its time?'

'For a period it would just observe. It didn't start talking to me or attacking me until I was in my teens. Up to that point it was just my silent follower. An inescapable companion.'

'Why would you say "companion" if it is your jailer?'

'It's had to endure this journey alongside me; like me, it had no choice in the matter. It was chosen just like I was. The only difference is that I believe it's happy in his role.'

'How so?'

'It does it without question, without deviation. It makes no pretence to what it is. It isn't my friend, nor does it want to be. At first I thought it was my protector, but it's become clear over the years that the only thing it was protecting me from was those who could derail me from the fate I have been given.'

'So it prevented you from deviating from the path so to speak?'

'Exactly. Anyone who tries to tamper with what the darkness has planned feels its touch, and it's never a pleasant experience. It's the touch of despair, a black wave of depression creeping across your eternal self. It feeds off whoever it can when it's not beneficial feeding from me.'

'How does it "feed"?'

'It drains happiness, sucks it dry revealing the emptiness of existence, the bleakness of eternity, the glory of suicide.'

'I thought you believed there was nothing after life.'

'That's why I said "glory". Suicide is the glorious escape from what it makes you feel, but it's a lie. It lies, it teases you with the notion of freedom then snatches it away whatever decision you make. You choose life, you exist in pain; you choose death, you exist in pain. There is no happy ending for the cancer that is mankind.'

'So it is depressive? Could it be simply that you, yourself, project a sense of melancholy that others pick up on?'

'I am not depressed. Are you suggesting that I make others depressed?'

'Not at all, but negativity is infectious, more so than happiness. Happy moods can be easily destroyed by one negative thought; whereas one happy thought rarely lightens a negative.'

'So you're suggesting that I ruin the happiness of others?'

'I am not suggesting anything, Daniel. I was offering it as a viewpoint. That what you perceive as the shadow causing it, may in fact be due to your negative thoughts.'

'That I'm to blame because you don't believe in the shadow's existence? That all this is imagined or self-created because it doesn't fit with the ways of your world? If that is what you are saying then why should I even bother to continue? Let's just conclude for your benefit that all this is bullshit and be done with it.'

'I am trying to understand.'

'You're trying to enforce your way, your beliefs.'

'Could you not at least try and view it from my perspective?'

'What would be the point? I know it would be like trying to believe a lie. I've believed far too many lies in my life, and I certainly don't need to be blinded by another one. I know the truth of my life, who are you to turn it into a lie?'

'I am not trying to turn what you say into a lie. I am simply giving you a possible explanation.'

'An explanation to my "condition"?'

'Yes. That is all I can do. It is up to you how you take that.'

'I thought you wanted to understand.'

'I do, but I can only respond to that by telling you what I believe that experience could be caused by. You wanted the truth and I am giving it to you. I am not trying to lie to you, Daniel.'

'I'm not lying to you either.'

'I believe you.'

'How do you think it feels to constantly have your truth ripped apart, scrutinised and regurgitated into it being your fault? Can you imagine how that feels? Imagine if it happened to you. Imagine being told that everything you have lived through was nothing but the product of your "vivid internal world".'

'It must be horrible.'

'What makes it worse is that I know I'm right. That what I see is truth, the reality of it all. Some day you will all wake up and feel exactly what I feel and when that happens I can guarantee none of you will offer me an apology.'

'What if you realise the opposite?'

'That you're right?'

'Exactly.'

'Nothing you have said convinces me. You just hide behind your beliefs and teachings. You are all blind and nothing you say could convince me otherwise.'

'Okay.' She makes notes on her pad. 'You once asked me to help you. Do you still want that help?'

'I once believed you could help me. Help me get rid of the emptiness I feel, but now I doubt you could. You can't help what you don't understand. I am beyond help. I am beyond redemption.'

'Do you truly believe that?'

'I believe it because the shadow told me.'

'The shadow told you that you are beyond help?'

'It told me that I would never be free from the darkness; that is all there is.'

'Do you want to be free from it?'

'I want to be free from all of it. I want it all to end.'

'If you could be freed from just the darkness, do you think you would be happy? You have some things to live for.'

'Like what?'

'Your boyfriend.'

'Is it worth it?'

'I think you believe it is. You seem to keep fighting for him. For the relationship, and I don't believe it is just for the comfort or fear of being alone.'

'But the darkness will prevent it all. There isn't much time left for me.'

'I don't understand.'

'You wouldn't.'

'Try me.'

'Now is not the time to talk about this. It makes sense only at the end.'

'It obviously has some relevance to what we are talking about at the moment. Why isn't there much time left for you?'

'Everything is falling away from me. Shedding itself like a skin. Decaying, rotting. I will end up in a position of nothing; in the end, I'll die with nothing. Alone and with absolutely nothing.'

'Like?'

'I will lose my home. My sanctuary will be taken from me and there is nothing I can do to prevent that. That is the most important thing to me. Without it I might as well just be dead.'

'Why will you lose it?'

'I just will. I can sense it. I can feel that that will be the final nail in this coffin of existence, and once that is hammered through I will finally be laid to rest in a grave. This prison will rot and I'll exit into nothing.'

'I am sure things will not be as bad as you think.'

'I know for a fact they will. It's the way everything in this life has worked out. I am entitled to nothing and nothing is all I shall receive. What more is there for something as meaningless as me?'

'More than you think.'

'You're lying.'

She makes notes. Pauses. Sighs. 'Can we take the subject away from this and look into the history of your shadow in a bit more depth. Maybe it will help me understand why you have such conviction in what it says.'

'It might help you understand but I doubt it would make you believe.'

'Understanding can help with belief.'

'Okay. So what do you want to know?'

'Let's go back to what you said about it at first only being observant, when did that change? When did the shadow start to talk to you?'

'When I was a teenager.'

'How old do you think you were?'

'Maybe thirteen. That feels about right. I can picture that moment but not the exact date. Its first words were only my name. Like it had finally been able to work its vocal cords in this world.'

'What happened?'

'I was sat in school. It was during an art lesson, I know it wasn't whilst I was sat in a formal setting.' He pauses, trying to picture the scene in his head. 'Yeah, I'd just been sat there daydreaming and it cut through like an alarm cuts through sleep. It was a whispered "Daniel". It was whispered right against my ear. It was like it was close enough to kiss it but didn't leave a give-away breath of air.'

'Could it have been anyone around you?'

'No. It was too deep, sounded too old. I jolted and looked around but there was no visible cause, but then I felt its presence. It was so alien in that space. It had kept itself private for years, but in that one whispered name I knew it was watching me in public again.'

'Had you seen it in public before?'

'When I was younger; before I went to high school. So up until I was ten it used to show itself.'

'Did you tell anyone?'

'I used to incorporate it into stories, to try and see if others saw it. At primary school, when I was in the infants, it used to stand in a corner on the school playing field, used to shield itself behind a fence and amongst bushes. My friends never used to be able to see it so I guess it became kind of a childhood game. An imaginary villain.'

'A villain?'

'They made it one out of what I said, although at that time I always associated it with neutrality.'

'Then when you grew up what happened?'

'When I moved to the juniors, it set up home in a ditch we claimed as a base called the "big dip". It always had an unnatural coldness about it. An unnerving stillness no matter what the season.'

'And these public appearances stopped when?'

'That moment in the rain. After that it took a step back. Faded away into the shadows that call corners of rooms their homes. It faded like a memory. Remembered but always in the past. Something that could be talked about, even jokingly.'

'Do you think its return was triggered by anything?'

'Thirteen was the age I was when I decided that I wanted to write as some form of career.' He pauses. 'Maybe it needed the absence of its presence to lure me into thinking the desire to write was born from my own choosing. Then once that had been established it swept back to remind me that I was not alone. Part of the plan was complete and the stage was set for the rest.'

'Did you feel that the words were being poured into your head at that stage?'

'No, but ideas did appear out of nothing, always along the same theme: one person's destruction of a world. I knew when I heard it speak directly to me for the first time that it was something important.'

'Directly?'

'I guess in a way I've always heard its voice internally, but in that moment it was outside. It was free.

'Okay. Had there ever been any preceding "outside" contact?'

'Only once. My brother and I caught a voice on a tape recording. It scared us shitless. It sounded demonic, a language unknown to our ears. It took over the whole recording. Leaving its message. It started with what sounded like wind and then it begun. Even to this day I've never forgotten what it sounded like. I never will. It was the voice of the darkness.'

'How old were you?'

'Ten.'

'Was the voice you heard spoken into your ear the same voice?'

'Similar. It had the same tones only less aggressive, and it spoke my name in English.'

'After the initial name, how often did he speak with you?'

'Then, not that often. It increased more when I was seventeen onwards. It still prefers to observe. When it speaks it is usually when something is going to deter me from the task I have to fulfil.'

'Do you want to tell me about any more experiences with it? Any that you consider to be extremely relevant?'

'If you want me to. I dunno where to start from.'

'Maybe from after it spoke to you.'

'Things changed after I heard it.'

'How do you mean?'

'Once I'd made the choice that I wanted to be an author, everything began to get blocked. It was like the personality I had built up over the years began to rot. Fall away like a suit of lies, revealing gradually the true fact of my life: that I am nothing but what I was put here to be. The darkness ripped off the shroud of what I thought I was and I was left lost. By the time I was fifteen I knew nothing. I didn't know who I was. I was alone in the emptiness that I now know is the only constant in this pathetic existence.' He pauses.

'We'll return to your feeling of emptiness again later if that is okay. I'm pretty confident of the link between your shadow and your inner sense of being empty, but at the moment I want to understand your shadow experiences more. Do you think you can remain focused?'

He nods.

'Okay then, let's continue.'

# FOURTEEN

The room itself is dark, or rather it wants to be dark but he never closes his bedroom door or curtains, so ambient light filters in like a pathetic city night sky. He turns in his bed, keeping his eyes closed as he does. He knows what he'll see when he opens them.

'You are awake,' a whisper in his ear.

He jolts upright. Glances round the room, heart pounding. The room sits empty. He falls back onto the bed. Closes his eyes and curls himself into a ball.

Silence.

Silence.

He turns to face the wall.

'Don't trust someone simply on what you see.' The voice again.

He begins to sing songs in his head to fill it with noise. The voice doesn't come again. Sleep does the same.

The next night his eyes open at the same time. He sees the shadow standing in its corner. He can feel its gaze upon him; can see the tendrils of smoke pouring around it, reaching for him. 'What do you want?' he screams at it. 'What the fuck do you want?'

He feels like the shadow just smirked at him, he can't see for definite but the small intake of air usually associated with that facial motion hit his ears. The shadow fades from sight.

'You fucking cunt,' he shouts at the empty space before falling back down onto the bed. He stares at the ceiling. His mind blank. He stares into a void.

Hands around his throat. Sudden pressure squeezing, thumbs digging in on either side of his Adam's apple. The blank, featureless face of the shadow stares down at him. 'Now is not your time, but it is coming. First you will break and from then your existence shall be shattered.'

Gone. All pressure removed. He is alone, panicking for air. He wants to scream but his throat is too sore. He sits up, slides out of bed and closes his bedroom door. A window is opened and he draws a cigarette from the packet and works it into his mouth. Click. Flame. Inhale. He exhales slowly as he looks outside through the glass.

'You will never be free,' the voice whispers into his ear. 'You will never be free.'

Inhale. Exhale. He sees a drop of condensation fall from below his ghostly reflection's eye. He refuses to accept that it's his own.

'It's always told me that I'll never be free. Its grip is too tight. It's the noose around my neck and any form of escape causes it to tighten until I relent and return.'

'Have you tried to be free?'

'Yes, doesn't every slave try to escape? But every time I've failed. All avenues blocked and I end up broken with nothing.'

'Could it be that you sabotaged your own escapes due to your own insecurities? That your fear of rejection is too great that you cause the rejection.'

'No, each blockage has been out of my hands. It was not of my doing. The decision was made by others. The doors closed in my face. The only way forward was through the doorways where the darkness' influence would be heard. Music, writing, drawing. All of these governed over and directed. These are my only successes and even those were minimal.'

'They are your talents.'

'Like I said before, I am a fraud. These are all the skills I have but have no control over. I can only create what the darkness commands.'

She sighs. Remains silent.

'What was that sigh for?' he asks.

'Do you want an answer even though you will dismiss it as a mere textbook conclusion?'

'You mean your answer to my "condition"?'

'An answer, or a possibility. I'm still trying to understand but they all lead back to the same point. One which I have already explained.'

'So I'm wasting your time?'

'Did I say that, Daniel? Does it feel like you are wasting my time?'

He shrugs. 'You're paid no matter how much or little I say.'

'That is true, but that is not why I am here. I am trying to understand like I said.'

'By the time I was seventeen it was ready to break me down. Once again I lost everything. I had no friends; I was constantly by myself. No one cared about me; yeah, quite literally no one gave a fuck. I'd become this thing that wasn't me. I'd lost control of this machine and the darkness let me. Words came out of my mouth that I would never say. I was pushed to the side-lines whilst I watched some other person take the steering wheel and wreck the last parts of my existence. Bringing an end to that era. The phoenix erupting into flames. Then there was nothing.'

He stares into the mirror. He doesn't know what is staring back at him. That face. That body. None of them are his. He doesn't look like that; how could he look like that? How could that ugly machine represent him to the greater world? It's worthless; it's dirt. He hates it. The very sight of it makes him want to cry.

He calls out for the shadow; calls into the darkness for an answer but none is given. His existence invaded by the creature looking back at him from within the glass. He hates it. Hates it. Hates it. Hates it. He slashes at its chest with the scalpel, watching the blood begin to redden its pale skin. The sight frenzies him; its passive acceptance spurs him on. Slash after slash he brings the scalpel down against the monstrosity, before soon he is a panting mess and the figure's body is a mass of ripped flesh from its collarbone down to its groin.

The figure continues to stare him in the eye.

He feels something trickle down his chest. He drops the scalpel and raises the hand to touch it. The figure does the same. He raises the hand to his eye level; the figure does the same. His fingers are covered in blood. He looks down and sees his damaged torso. He looks back at the figure in the mirror. His reflection does the same.

With a sob he falls to the floor. Foetal position. He tries not to cry. He doesn't succeed.

'So, you were completely unaware that you were actually harming yourself?'

'The person I cut was not me. It did not look like me. It still doesn't. I guess that was the first time I fully realised I was a prisoner inside this stolen body.'

'Do you think the fact that you felt empty could have caused or effected this? You have a history of dissociation.'

'No, the feeling of being nothing was the necessity that the darkness required. It severed the false notion that I was a complete person with a correct soul in the correct body. Although it had directed my life to that point, it needed me to make myself aware of my separation. This was the moment I cut that falsehood and realised I was different. That I was a prisoner, but at that point I didn't realise what my purpose was. I just knew I wanted to write. To be an author.'

'How did you feel at first about your absolute certainty that you were in a way separate from your body?'

'I'd always felt a separation, but I knew then that I was not separate from *my* body, I was simply in the wrong body. As to how I felt, well, I dunno. I guess things made a little bit more sense.'

'How so?'

'The aversion to mirrors or reflections; the way people treated me like I was different. I've always believed that something about my eyes gave me away. I think people could see the disconnection before I did.'

'There could be a truth in the last part. People do pick up on things like that, differences. It doesn't define you as a person though.'

'This does define me. I am different. I'm not meant to be here. I've tried so many times to be somebody, to fit in, to be a part of your world. Each time I've failed.'

'Have you tried being yourself?'

'Look at where that has led me. Be what is expected, I fail. Be what I want, fail. Be what the darkness wants, a long road straight into the distance. No direction, just forward; waiting for the corner to arrive but it never comes. Fail, fail, or wait. Constantly on hold. Write, write, write, but get nothing; a few readers, all affected by what I write but it's not enough.'

'Enough for who?'

'Me. I want it to take off, then I'll be closer to my freedom.' He turns away, holding back his emotion.

'Can I go back a bit? I can understand failing whilst trying to be someone who you are not, but how do you fail whilst being yourself?'

'It's a double life. I know why I am here, why I was taken from the void and put here. I know I'm just expected to focus on my task. That is all both the shadow and the darkness want, but...' He pauses again, bites on his lip. 'But...'

'But you want something more.'

He eyes move, trying to find something to settle on.

'You want someone.'

He looks her in the eyes and lets the emotion free. 'I want someone... I want someone who can understand.' He cries openly. 'I just want someone to love me.'

# FIFTEEN

The argument had been brutal. Words spat out without thought of any consequence, without any thought of the cuts they would rip into the fabric of the moment. A moment. The murder of love; its corpse left on the ground.

Surrounded by the destruction of anger, reality sets in. Smashed glasses and plates are replaceable, tables and chairs can be returned to their legs. Feelings cannot. *What have I done? Why do I do it? What now?* The usual questions, the usual emptiness. Head in hands, he cries. Emotion unrestrained and exiting with the force that only comes from hurting the one person you care most about in the world. *Fuck. Fuck. Fuck.*

Where does it go from here? The unknown. Is his other half feeling the same? Does he care? He hopes he does. He hopes he will fight for this as much as he is trying to. Follow your heart. Listen to it and if that person means the world to you, cling on to it. Hold on to its slipping grip and try and pull them back from over the edge of the cliff. Never give in. Never give up. Never give in to fear.

Fear. That's all he can feel. Once again losing everything and opening himself to the cold realisation that he had gone too far. Taken one step over the line and brought the whole world crashing down. *Shit.* He prays to God. He doesn't believe in Him but in this one moment, he wishes He existed, listened and helped.

How can anything be the same again? Was the love they had as strong as they had thought? He knows his is, but who can ever be certain of the other? Too many questions. Always too many questions without answers. Questions solved through experience, through sitting down and speaking. What if it's beyond speech? That's a question he doesn't want to know the answer to.

Both had hurt the other, each had pulled out knives and sliced the other. There was no innocent party, there was no right. There was no need for any of this. Both had found out each other's dark side. *Sweet fucking Jesus Christ, please let me know forgiveness. Slut Mother Mary, please embrace us. Dear blind God, for once let everything work out for the best.*

An empty prayer from an emptying soul.

Silence.


'But you have someone who loves you.'

'And look what's happening there. I keep fucking it up. I try my hardest to stop, to not get stupid thoughts in my head, but…'

'You got hurt, Daniel, those feelings are natural.'

'I know, but I can't get the idea out of my head that it all happened because of me. Like if I was someone different, someone normal then none of this… none of this…' He breaks off. Sighs. 'If I was someone else, he would be happy.'

'Do you not think he's happy?'

'Who could be happy with me? No one has in the past. I've pushed them all away. I've fucked up on every relationship.'

'You obviously love him.'

'I do. I love him more than anything in the world. We've been through a lot and I've forgiven him for everything. Some people think I'm crazy, that I should have left him ages ago, but I can't.'

'Why not?'

'You have to fight for what you love. I love him. He's the only guy I've wanted. Like really wanted. Wanted from the minute, no second I laid eyes on him. And I've pushed him away. If not pushed, then pushing him away.' He smacks the side of his head. 'I'm a worthless fucking piece of shit. I'm what the darkness has made me. Love isn't meant for me. I'm not meant to be loved. No matter how much I want it. Eventually they all see that I am just a fucking ghost.'

'Do you feel loved?'

'As much as I understand how love feels.'

'Then why are you so upset?'

'Because… because I don't understand why; why anyone would want to love me.'

'Have you felt this love from your previous boyfriends?'

'Each time has felt different. Innocent; intense; fading; broken. Each time has had a different quality. Like that was, is how it's meant to be. Like I was put into those situations to experience them for the darkness' plans.'

'And the current?'

'It feels true. It grew so rapidly but naturally. It was never forced. It hasn't changed in how I feel no matter what has happened. It is constant. It's nice.'

'And you do not want to lose that?'

'Obviously. The darkness hates it, but in a way it benefits its aims. He actually supports what I do, that in turn makes me enjoy it. For the first time I actually enjoy transcribing the works of the dark.' He sighs. 'For once it doesn't seem so lonely.'

'Have the incidences with the shadow decreased since the relationship started?'

'They've increased.'

'In a positive way?'

'They've never been positive.'

'Never?'

'Well there was one case, but it makes no sense mentioning it now. It makes sense at the end.'

'Okay.' She makes a note on her pad; a reminder to return to it later. 'So, how have these experiences got worse?'

'More vivid. More aggressive. I think they're fucked off because I've found something, no, it's more than a thing; I've found someone who distracts me away from their influence.'

'Does it feel like they are flexing their muscle so to speak?'

'It's more a reminder of who is actually in control. Like a parent they've put a hand on my shoulder to remind me to stay focused.'

'Have you?'

'Do I have the choice?'

'I guess not. Has the darkness ever made its stance before with regards to any other boyfriend?'

'Once that I know of.'

'When was that?'

'When I was twenty-one.' He pauses. 'He chose to do it in one of the most fitting locations.'

'Where?'

'The house where it had watched over me for thirteen years.'

'What happened?'

'My brother had been depressed. It got worse when I arrived back with my boyfriend.'

'Do you think it was the shadow that made it worse?'

'I didn't at first. He used to walk from his room and just stare at his reflection in the bathroom mirror. You'd just see him stood there. God knows what he saw.'

'How did you react?'

'I didn't.'

'Did you say anything?'

'Only when my boyfriend told me to. He was concerned. Really concerned. So I spoke to my brother. I gave him the talk an older brother should give the younger.'

'And you are the younger?'

'Yes.'

'How did that feel?'

'I dunno. I was annoyed. He's my older brother, he's not meant to show signs of weakness.' He pauses. 'Anyway, just as we were almost done, my boyfriend bursts in shitting himself. He'd gone to the bathroom but as he'd turned on the light he'd seen the shadow rise from sitting on the side of the bath and reach for the light; when it touched it, the bulb blew. He'd never been told about the shadow before. He said it was like it had been waiting but the wrong person had entered.'

'What happened after?'

'We went out for a walk but the shadow followed us. It's like it was really fucked off. Not at me, or my brother. It was fucked off at my boyfriend for making me snap its hold over my brother, depriving it of a free feed. It tormented him, then that night as we slept, it spoke to me. It told me to get rid of him. I said "no." The reply was simple "then keep him away from our affairs." Then silence.'

'The aftermath?'

'My brother got happier. My boyfriend didn't see the shadow again. I was fed upon.'

'You got depressed?'

'I sacrificed a part of my happiness to protect those I loved. It was the only way. I couldn't lose either. I couldn't return to my solitude. I figured each would result in unhappiness; at least this way I could retain something. From then that's how it's been maintained.'

'Maintained?'

'I know I'm not here to be happy, and that whenever I am, the darkness will suck it dry until all that is left is a bitter memory. So I don't let it. I give it my happiness. I protect those I love.'

'But I thought your aim was to let the darkness into the minds of mankind.'

'And it will, eventually. I've damaged everyone I've got close to, or have almost done so. It's inevitable. Most of mankind can rot, but some... some I like too much to hurt... but as I said, the darkness will inevitably touch them, and once that task has been achieved they will leave to pass it on to another.' He smirks. 'I don't believe my legacy is filled with kind words.'

'You believe everyone hates you?'

'I'm a cancer. It's not a matter of love and hate. It's a case of removal and prevention.'

'Why then do you get so upset when you are removed?'

'Who wouldn't? No matter how bad a person you are, you'll always feel a pain at rejection.'

'True.'

'End of the day, the shadow does not want anyone to stand in the path of the darkness. The darkness wants it to be this way, and from all of this talking I can now see that everything is pathetic when stood against that.'

'Are you saying none of this has helped?'

'Yes.'

'And is not helping?'

'That's the same question. All any of this has done is given me a chance to finally tell my story.' He pauses. 'No, not story. It's allowed me to clear out my secrets and as a result put everything into its pitiful place. It has revealed truths. Mainly one truth, but for that you need to decide what it is.'

'Things can change. I still believe that all this is a part of a broken subconscious. It can, with time and effort, all be pieced back together. The future could be so much more than what you believe.'

He laughs. 'Things don't change for me. Don't you think I've tried? Nothing is in my control, not one bit. All the chess pieces are played by other hands and it's a game that I am not included in. You can be sure of nothing in this world. No, I lie. You can be sure of *one* thing. Do not trust anyone. Now you can sit there and tell me that that is born out of continual bad experiences, but deep down you know that I'm right and the only reason you won't accept it as a set in stone basis of all existence is because it would topple your world; it would break it apart at its seams and crumble you to dust like it has me. Instead you tell me that I created this life I lived; that I filled it with these experiences and pain. Ask yourself the question I keep asking. Who would create such an existence? Who would be stupid enough to? I can only speak from what I've lived and I have seen this world for what it truly is. Once you've seen its rotten core, there is absolutely no way you could ever return to seeing it for what you say it to be, no matter how hard you could try.

'There is nothing but greed and self-obsession. Life is solitary and as such you all try to make it as cosy and warm as you can, but tell me one thing. Can you truly ever know with one hundred percent certainty what anyone else is doing when they are not with you? And more importantly can you truly know what they think when they are?'

'No, but that is where trust comes in.'

'Trust is, as I've said, just another word for ignorance. There is no certainty in trust. Mankind lies on a daily basis. Trust cannot exist, no matter how hard anyone tries.'

'I disagree.'

'You would. So tell me, you said that everything I experience is a fiction; that the shadow and the darkness are just my creation. If that is the case then how could the following have happened? One of my friends was offering to use magic to get me and my ex-boyfriend back together again, and when I say "magic", I'm not talking hocus-pocus, I'm talking *real* magic, the art of manipulation. As he was offering this to me, at the same moment we both heard the voice of my shadow bellow "no". We heard it from the same physical direction but saw nothing. How could that have happened if it was merely something that existed in my world?'

She says nothing.

'How could the shadow tell me someone's father who was believed to be dead was "not dead but in Japan" months before this was actually proven to be the case?'

She says nothing.

'And once again, how could the same shadow, on the first day of January, tell me that on the thirteenth of November that same year a tragic event would take place? Then on that exact day someone who was like a grandparent to me died. That's a hell of a lot of coincidences I created there, and yet it always happens.'

She says nothing.

'So if all of my existence is created by me, then I seem to have one hell of a power over the rest of the "real" world in which I'm forced to exist. So I'm either a fucking prophet, or the more likely explanation is that everything is predestined to happen and the darkness knows all of this.'

She sighs. 'So you believe you can predict the future?'

'I've told you that things that I was told would happen, which were out of my direct influence, actually took place. I think that's more a case of premonition than prediction.'

'So you think everything is predetermined?'

'I don't think, I know. Nothing is truly in our control. I can see it. I've experienced it. I always know when something has happened. I can sense it. That is something the darkness has allowed me. The only thing it keeps secret are the details of my own existence. Well, that was until recently.'

'How so?'

'The shadow once told me it would only show me its face when my end was coming, and has kept its identity secret. However, the last time it strangled me it was different. Its head had more definition. It wasn't just its usual human shaped shadow. It had formed into the shadow of a dog's head. Y'know, kinda like a Doberman. It was still featureless but it was the first time since I've seen it that its form has changed. It felt as though I was being made aware that the time was coming.'

'How did you feel about that?'

'Scared. It freaked me out more than it normally would. It seemed so monumental. Then a few nights later, I saw the shadow again, but it was sat at the edge of my bed waiting for me to wake. For the first time it was kind to me. It spoke as though we were friends.'

'What did it say?'

'It told me the day that all this will end.'

'I do not follow.'

'It told me the day that I will die.'

'And this was that positive time you mentioned earlier?'

'Yes.'

'Have you seen it since?'

'I've seen it but it hasn't touched me. It feels like everything is winding down. My whole life preparing for that approaching moment.'

'How does that make you feel?'

'At peace. I wasn't scared by what it said.'

'Peace?'

'Yeah, I've been praying for years for all this to end; to be freed from all this pain, and now it told me when my freedom is coming.'

'And you believed it'

'What reason would I have not to?'

'What if it does not happen?'

'Then I'm sure something will end.'

'So the shadow did not say you would die?'

'It told me to tie up all loose ends by 1:10pm on that day as that is the moment it all ends. I take that as a clear indication of what is to occur.'

'Maybe it is the moment they will leave you.'

He smiles. 'For that to be the case, you'll have to admit that they are sentient beings independent of my control.'

She doesn't reply.

'You could never accept that viewpoint could you? Not even the slightest glimpse into acknowledging it. Such a closed mind. I tell you now that everything you believe is a falsehood created for you by those who want to control you, and you follow like sheep. Such a blinded existence. I would pity you but all I can feel for your pathetic race is disgust. I could never be part of your world even if I wanted to. Such a goddamned shit hole of existence. An existence governed by days. Pay days, bill days, holidays,

Friday piss ups, weekends off, and then back to work again. Are you truly satisfied knowing that the only time you'll get to enjoy your world is when you're old and frail, and that's all dependent upon whether or not you reach that point.' He shakes his head. 'Such a pitiful existence.'

'That is unfortunately the way of the world.'

'That is unfortunately the way in which you justify your slavery.'

She makes a note on her pad. 'We have to agree to disagree.'

'There is no need for us to agree to anything, for the simple fact you believe that there is no true basis for my existence for you to feel the need to actively disagree on. You believe I'm merely crazy and disconnected from reality and no matter what I say it will be dismissed as a symptom of psychosis. All of this has been for nothing at the end of the day.'

'It has not been for nothing. I have a greater understanding of your condition.'

'There you go again. My "condition". Don't you mean your label for me? Place me into the box and let someone else deal with it. At the end of the day, you have failed. You have done nothing to help other than confirm what I already know: that mankind is just a deaf, blind species that can't move beyond the accepted constructs of its manipulated society.'

'I have not failed.'

'You have, and you know that I'm definitely right about that. What have you achieved other than prove your own inability to change someone? You've met your match and to me you aren't even a worthy opponent.'

'You believe that you are here to change people's minds, to open them to "the darkness" and yet you have not changed my opinion. By your own definition of failure, you have failed too.'

'But I haven't. How many times did my questioning of your world cause you to change the subject? How many times couldn't you answer back? All those moments unnerved you as it made you question; it might have only been a split millisecond of doubt but it was there and it scared you. In that one tiny moment a bit of the darkness crawled through that crack and entered deep within you. Those small doubts will be revisited and re-dismissed, but with each re-visitation the void will grow. I made you question what was meant to be set in stone, you have to live with that.'

'I changed the subject as we were moving away from what we should have been discussing.'

'What if I brought them up now? Now that is it the subject we are discussing?'

'This is not relevant?'

'How so? It's what we're discussing. I'm not leading a subject away from anything.'

She closes her notepad and looks at the clock. 'That is us for today.'

He smirks. 'Really?'

'Daniel, the session is over.'

# SUICIDE NOTE

## SIXTEEN

Tired. I'm so fucking tired. At first I thought there could have been a way in which some of this pain could be eased, but everything has been made clear. There is no help for me. There never was. It was all an illusion that was offered to lure me into the control of your world. A world so closed to the prospect of anything that goes against what is dictated as truth. A world blind to the darkness that surrounds us all and is awakening to end the disease that is mankind. The end is coming for your mortal frames, but for your souls an eternity of pain awaits. I wish I could say I was sorry for you, but the truth is simply that I am not. If I was God, this world would have been dust years ago.

So, what should I write upon these pages? What worth would they offer to your world of lies other than some form of confirmation that the labels and names of my so-called 'conditions' were accurate? You could take it as an indication of that, or you could take it as it is: a final attempt to make you understand why this shortening of my already short remains of this existence was the only option. This was my choice. This is my selfish action. The first thing I have done for myself. The first time I am truly standing up to the shadow and the darkness that it serves. I know the result will be the punishment of my soul but the freedom from this rotten form that has been my prison for twenty-nine years is worth even that, and I am ready for it.

The truth is that every time I close my eyes I can just see the lie, but I guess that's the only truth I have ever known. How can anyone move on from that? It's like your world is one big game, and because I was never given the chance to play, everything has just been shit. I know I haven't been in control, but when you filled my head with your explanations you placed an idea in there that all this could have been different. I know for a fact it couldn't but that notion created a fantasy and now all I feel is a never-ending jealousy for what could have been, and now I'm too old to enjoy it, too bitter. Too jaded. It's an interesting fantasy but that's all it could ever be. Your world is a lie; the fantasy happiness is a lie. I've seen the truth and from that there is no escape. So each and every time I try to turn, the only way is down into this misery and filth. I've long since stopped thinking about salvation.

I'll spare you all the longwinded history of my life and settle simply with a mere mention of its continuous theme. I've never been happy, there's always been something lying in wait to steal it from me. So with that in mind, you will hopefully accept that I stayed for a lot longer than any of you would have had you been in my shoes. I'm a strong person, but eventually even the strong break. To recover you need hope, and for me there is clearly no hope in getting better, or being fixed, or even being able to be part of your world. I've broken in the past and tried to pick up the pieces, but it is clear that there is nothing in this worthless existence that is going to change in my favour. There is only so many times you can bang your head against the same brick wall until you realise that. I know the shadow told me the day I die, but I simply couldn't wait those few months, so, as I've already mentioned, I will take my stand against it. The darkness may have controlled my whole life, but my death will be my own decision. My choice. My exit. My conclusion.

Could any of you fathom my situation, my existence? Would you want to? To have no control over your own life. Dying each and every day in a body that is not your own. I've heard all the explanations, all the verbal bullshit poured out at me in an attempt to explain how I fit into the rules of your world. I've sat and listened to how my entire existence has been dismissed as little more than a malfunctioning brain. So let's look at my 'situation' from your world's perspective and see if that makes you understand on your terms. Imagine being told that everything, your whole fucking world has been shaped by a psychosis. That you're so fractured that in some cases there is no connection at all. That what makes you *you* is ingrained so much with the 'fantasies' that to remove them would be to remove you. Imagine being told that the only help you have is to be given ways to cope with the 'illusions' that have caused the very reasons why you want to die. The doors to reality are locked for the simple reason that your sickness developed at such a young age that you never experienced it in the first place. Forever destined to be the outsider no matter what you try to do to be otherwise. Then, knowing all that explanation, seeing it as a view point, being unable to even entertain the notion that your creativity comes from somewhere in you and not from the darkness you know has been playing your life like a fiddle. Imagine, just for me, what that must feel like. The intensity of that situation. Imagine being told that you will never get truly better. Then imagine you are given the notion that it could have all been different. I doubt any of you could even do that adequately. I mean, whilst you were running around playing Cowboys and Indians, or dressing up your teddy bears ready for their tea party, I was creating a whole new reality. I've created a world, what have you achieved above normality? When you die, the reality you hold with a cast iron fist will soldier on without you. When I die, my entire world dies with me. Or rather that's what you believe. I, however, know that my task to plant the seeds of darkness into your pathetic existence will have had some effect, and in my absence the weeds will slowly germinate and consume the very thing that chose to lock me out. My only regret is that I will not be here to see it; that and the fall of your stone messiah of science. One small regret from a lifetime of mistakes.

In death we shall share a common ground. We all rot in the end.

So when the shadows come for me, please pray only in silence. They come only to claim what is theirs. My existence will fade away and leave only this ugly body as a memory. A memory that like anything else will fade even more into nonexistence with the death of a generation. I'll leave a legacy for which there will be no memory of the saviour's name.

No one can judge that which they were not a part of.

There has been but one thing I have strived for, that I hope was controlled by me, and that was my desire to be loved, and I believe that I found it, in my own understanding of it at least. I know I've loved. I guess I've been loved. All of them shared one thing in common. All of them grew tired of me before I did them, and I let all of them walk away, well all except one. The last one. No matter what he did, I continued; the trust rotting away until all that remained was a thin membrane of little more than anticipation for the next lie. And then, sure enough, as expected, that 'trust' was broken. Once again he slipped and his dick slid into another random guy's mouth. But I guess that is the only thing I learnt about your world, or rather it's the one thing you all neglect. Sometimes you have to truly put aside everything and fight for who you love. It's so easy to run from the first upset, the first hurt. I guess the reason we lasted so long is due to my failure of trust. This proves that you can have a relationship without trust. So, let me hear your argument for that. The fact of the matter is simple: if I had trusted him I would have lived in ignorance. Trusting him would not have prevented him from cheating, nor would it have changed anything. Ignorance may be bliss to you, but for me I can't be happy unless I know the truth.

This is, I guess, my one achievement in this life. I fought for love. I had it slap me in the face, had it spit and shit on me, but in one instance I fought for it and never gave up. I stayed when all of you would have walked away. Does that make me an idiot? Probably, but as you can no doubt see, happiness was not meant for me. I realised far too late that I should have simply been happy in my unhappiness.

Anyway, I digress. I'm rambling away from the point and somehow hoping that you'll suddenly understand. I know, however, you will not. This isn't for my benefit to write this. I mean at the end of the day, your world locked me out, I was never a part of it, so why now, in my passing, should I make my death appear understandable within it? I've lived my entire life locked in a prison; a prison in your world. So let this bodily prison die in the world it was born just as it had existed: empty. It was born an empty shell, so it dies that way. I was placed within it against my will, now on its demise I can return to the other side. My true existence had no part in your world and nor will my death. I've done my time. I've served my sentence.

Now you have what your world needs to justify my demise. I hope it fills your criteria, your boxes and your emotional states. I hope it gives a meaning to something that is meaningless. So, count your days. The day is coming. I have seen what awaits you all. I have seen your eternity. Embrace the pain when it arrives; doing so will make it that little bit more bearable.

The darkness is coming. You have all been warned. My piece has been played.

This, whatever it is, is over.

## CONVERSATION V

# SEVENTEEN

'Do you know what this will mean?'

Daniel opens his eyes and sits up. 'I think I do.'

'And you think that you have a choice?' The shadow stands in the doorway. Tall, gaunt. Tendrils of black smoke rising and falling around it. In the silence that follows its question it moves slowly towards the edge of the bed and sits down. They stare at each other. Neither says a word.

'What else can I do?' Daniel breaks the silence.

'You can do what you've always done. Continue.'

'Why would I want to? What would be the point? I'm tired. Tired of all this noise. Tired of being a prisoner. Tired of this existence. Surely after all this time you're tired as well?'

'I never tire. It is true that it has been my duty to watch over you; to lead you to this point, just as I have lead you to many others. It has been a journey shared but for which I feel nothing. I know who you are, where you come from. I've known your destiny from the start. Everything planned and now you think you can suddenly choose the ending?'

'Does that scare you? To not be in control?'

'Scare me?' A pause. 'No. You've had these thoughts in the past; a rebel streak we hadn't expected, but we adapted, we learnt. Even as the prisoner to a machine your true self seeped through and took over. So maybe you could find some solace in that. We didn't make you who you are; just what you are. Your personality and desires were yours alone. We just took away all opportunities. We knew you'd choose to write, but that choice was yours and it fitted so well into our plan. Granted the output is ours, but the will is yours. You couldn't have stopped writing our words even if you tried. You enjoy it too much.'

'So you've used me. All this time I've been used by both their world and yours.'

'That is truth.'

'So how could any of this be down to me?'

'We never guided your love. We knew how important that was to you. You found that on your own.'

'But how could it have been on my own? You guided me into those situations as they offered you something you needed me to experience.'

'We placed you; you adapted and found the person you needed. As much as we did not want to, we let that person accompany you as we learnt that is what you needed. Had it been left to us you would have existed alone.'

'So it was real?'

'Everything anyone has done to you has been because they wanted to do it; we did not guide their hand. We did this because we needed you to see the truth of mankind. And you did. You saw it and for years wanted to prove us wrong. You had such a will to live that we extended your existence. We slowed our plans and moved our deadlines.'

'What?'

'You've felt it. You know at which point you should have died. You've always known, even as a child.'

'That I was meant to die at twenty-five?'

'That is correct. You were only meant to be on this earth for twenty-five years. I would ask "did you not notice how even more meaningless it all became after that age?" But I know you know the answer. You had no opportunities to work for you simply because there was nothing the world had left to offer; you weren't meant to be here. You continued through will alone.'

'That was when my dreams stopped. The emptiness in their absence was so unbearable. I remember. I remember wanting to die so much, wanting to just end it all. No one was listening; it was so cold, just screaming at the dark.'

The shadow remains silent.

'I wanted to die so fucking much. Then I saw you in that dream. You advised me. For the first time you helped.'

'I gave advice. On that day I too broke the rules. I saw your struggle, that strength of will inside you. I wanted to see what you could do. You surprised us all. You broke the darkness' plan and you did it for one reason; your usual reason. You chose to live because of love; your need to feel a love that you had spent all your years desiring. You felt it once, but you wanted the next level of it. Love prevented your death.'

'So, are you here for the same reason?'

'No. I can offer no words this time. You have achieved your personal goal. You have found to love without trust. There is nothing more powerful than that. There is nothing more about love you can learn.'

'So you're saying there is nothing for me?'

'There was nothing for you after twenty-five. I am saying there is nothing to keep that will of yours aflame.

As with everything, I know that you know this too.' The shadow places a cold hand on his leg. 'So tell me. Have you found what you wanted?' A pause. 'Learnt what you needed to?'

Daniel sighs. 'I don't know. You're right though. It all feels empty now. This love. I can feel it. It feels just as strong as that first time I experienced it; if not stronger. The more that trust got broken, the more I wanted to hold on to it. I can't let it go. Everything has snowballed to this point and now it all feels empty. Meaningless. Maybe I have proved to myself that the emotion of love is so powerful, and that it can be experienced without trust, but now it just feels dead. Love entwined with the expectation of the next slip up. Happiness waiting for the pain from the desires of another. Maybe love without trust is so much easier than love with trust in a way. You can move on. Hold disappointment towards one person rather than having to start again and learn to love someone new, only for them to shit on you.' He pauses. 'I want to believe that he felt the same for me as I him, but I can't. If he did he wouldn't have done what he did. He satisfied my entire love and desire, but I couldn't do the same for him. So I live with that. It hurts. Love hurts. That is what I learnt. It hurts more than anything you have put me through. It is a horrible emotion. I hate it.'

'You hate it but you fought for it. You wanted it so much that it clouded everything else.'

'Who doesn't want to be loved? Who doesn't want to feel needed? I did. I have. Now I'm empty. There's nothing to fight for.'

'You have lost the will?'

'The will for anything. They have called our world a fiction, but they are wrong. It is their world that is fiction. Everything within it is built on lies, and that was one thing no one told me the answer to. How once all the little lies come to the fore, the entire experience becomes a falsehood. Take my boyfriend for example. The more I learn, the more he as a person mutates into a stranger before my eyes. Burnt from the ground up. My perception had been based on a lie. Half-truths. So what does that make the person you loved? A ghost. An illusion. Things fall into place. The jigsaw is completed and what then? Accept what you had believed or the true image in front of your eyes? How are you meant to cope with that? Too much of my life has been dismissed as a lie, and now one of my realities can be dismissed in the same way. Did I love a person or an imagination? The one thing I thought to be true gets eaten away and once again I am alone. He was the foundation of my connection to their world, and now I am left thinking what was really there. A pretence; another false door to nowhere. And yet I still love the person I "knew". No matter how jaded the viewpoint, that "person" still exists and even though I know otherwise I cannot separate the two.'

'And does this also apply to their world as a whole?'

'Like I said, their world is based on lies. Lies are not fact, and what is not fact is fiction. Their world has labelled me, tried to destroy my truth with lies. They have given me this notion that it never had to be this way. A million alternatives have flooded into my head and created all these "what ifs" and "maybes". I know it couldn't have been different; that this is how it should have been, but to have all those doubts kills you. Their world has given me a choice, but in that gift they stole my meaning.'

'Your meaning is to fulfil our task.'

'My meaning was to help the darkness enter into this world. It was to help bring about the destruction of that hideous race. Mankind needs to burn, and as I told them, if I was God their world would be dust.'

'So how have they stolen that?'

'They have told me that it is all me. That all of this, you, the darkness, is all some figment of my own imagination. They have taken away the task I have to do for you and turned it into me. But they are wrong. They are all so fucking wrong.'

'They have quantified your experience in the only way they know how. They have fitted you into their box, or rather they have tried. That rebellious streak in you has confounded them as much as it has us. You are a powerful individual. That is something to be proud of. You have challenged the darkness, you have challenged reality, and you have challenged yourself.'

'And now I want it to end.'

'It doesn't just end. There is no end. Just as there is no beginning. There is only infinity. The fear.'

'Fear?'

'The unknown. You are born from nothing, you return to that nothing. But that nothing continues. You know the pain of the other side. You know this will not get better. You will never be free.'

'I know!' Daniel shouts; screams his anger into the shadowed face that has tormented him all his life. 'You all lied to me. No, the word "lie" would mean that I was actively seduced by your ways. I never had the choice. *You* pulled me out of the dark and threw me into this body; you mapped a twenty-five year story that didn't go according to plan. By your own admission you said I should have died at twenty-five. I was only meant to be here for twenty-five years and you continued that torture.'

'*You* continued.'

'You said that by twenty-five I should have achieved everything. That that was when I was meant to die.'

'But *you* didn't achieve. *You* didn't fulfil what was expected. *You* chose to fight against us for love, and *you* chose to continue living for the very same reason. Who are you to judge us?'

'So because I fought against you, because I slowed down your plans, because I…'

'You followed your heart.'

'What?'

'We never wanted you to find love. That was not what we had anticipated. *You*, your pathetic need to be loved is what derailed and destabilised the plan. Your love is the reason you are still here; still pushing on.'

'You're punishing me for wanting to be loved?'

'No, we saw what a powerful commodity it is.'

'What?'

'Yes love distracted you, but it also opened for us so many doors. It was a commodity we had overlooked. We showed you such pain; the filthy core of the human condition, but the weed of love created an emptiness in you that we hadn't expected. It intensified all of your other feelings. The pain you experienced because of it was far more that we predicted. You poor creature, had you not learnt to love you would have died when expected and been free. But now, now we simply can't let that power go.'

'So, let me try to understand. You're saying that if I had never fallen in love I would have been free.'

'Yes. It is love that keeps you here. Not the love of yourself, but the love you feel for another. You continue to exist in this Hell solely for the comfort they give you. And now, you are so in love that no matter what they do, you will fight for them. Your desire has removed our timeframe. We now know that you can endure so much more than we thought, so we chose not to let you be free.'

'This makes no sense. You're just twisting everything.'

'We are twisting nothing. There were no rules against this. No promises were broken. The body you control exists in their world. You exist in ours. You have no control over either. You are, as you've always been, a prisoner. Only now the game board is bigger.'

'And what if that, as you put it, "rebel streak" in me decides otherwise?'

'You won't.' The shadow stands up from the bed. 'We've been here before.'

'You said this time was different. That the "will" was no longer there.'

'The will is no longer there, that is clear for anyone to see, but I lied to you earlier. I said that there was nothing more about love you could learn. There is, and for you it will be the hardest thing in the world to even contemplate. You need to learn to love yourself. You are incapable of doing anything for yourself, always putting others first.

You say you don't want to exist but yet here we are having this conversation. So what is left in will's place? Belief. Belief that it could all get better; that it could all work out. Regardless of whether or not you agree, hope lurks somewhere inside you.

'No matter how much you want to fall, you will never hit the bottom. Here's a simple notion for you. Ever think that being in this situation is what we wanted?' The shadow turns and moves towards the doorway.

Daniel sits in silence.

Without turning the shadow continues. 'Nothing but the choice in the person you love is in your control. Remember that. Did you think I came here to comfort you? Did you think I came here to build your spirits? I came to tell you what I've told you before. You'll never be free.'

'But you told me it would all end.'

'I told you *it* will end, I did not specify what *it* was.'

Daniel jumps out of his bed and runs towards the shadow. It spins, smacking him around the face. As he falls back onto the bed, it jumps on him. Strangling him with its familiar grip.

'You will never be free,' its featureless face screams at him. 'You will never be free.' It explodes into thousands of flies.

Daniel jumps up. Breathing in sharply, his throat sore. He is alone. He crawls up the bed and under the covers. The flat is cold. It breathes in silence. He pulls a pillow closer and hugs it. A poor substitute for a person but he doesn't know what his boyfriend is doing or who he is with. He only knows the possibilities. He wants to know everything; to be in control of everything. He knows he is in control of nothing; not even his own existence.

He closes his eyes, praying for sleep. He has never felt so alone. He knows it will only get worse.

How can you end something if you can't even write its conclusion?